"Kiss me,"

Julianne demanded. "Kiss me and don't stop until…until…"

"We turn blue?" Tony said, feeling laughter and being surprised by it. Inside, he was serious, very serious.

"Until there's no more hunger," she whispered.

"If the hunger is satisfied, then we'll be lovers in every sense of the word," he warned her. "I'd kiss you until we both went crazy. If we were lovers."

"Yes," she cried softly. "Yes."

"Would you melt in my arms? Would you yield to me? Give me anything I want?"

She forced her weighted eyelids to open, to meet his challenging stare. "What we both want," she reminded him.

"If we were lovers," he said roughly.

"If we were lovers," she echoed in ement.

Dear Reader,

I found out how effective a coyote fence was the hard way—I backed into one while trying to get the best picture of an impressive rock formation. The fence was made from cactus canes nailed side by side on a wooden structure. My hostess, who had a lovely flower and vegetable garden, said it also kept rabbits and other critters from sneaking in and eating the plants. I asked how she got the cactus nailed up without getting stickers. Her answer: "Very carefully." I'm not saying this incident was the sole inspiration for Tony and Julianne's story, but it certainly seemed to fit into their investigative efforts!

Best,

Laurie Paige

UNDER THE WESTERN SKY

LAURIE PAIGE

SPECIAL EDITION®

Published by Silhouette Books

America's Publisher of Contemporary Romance

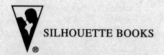 **SILHOUETTE BOOKS**

ISBN-13: 978-0-373-24781-3
ISBN-10: 0-373-24781-8

UNDER THE WESTERN SKY

Visit Silhouette Books at www.eHarlequin.com

Printed in U.S.A.

LAURIE PAIGE

"One of the nicest things about writing romances is researching locales, careers and ideas. In the interest of authenticity, most writers will try anything…once." Along with her writing adventures, Laurie has been a NASA engineer, a past president of the Romance Writers of America, a mother and a grandmother. She was twice a Romance Writers of America RITA® Award finalist for Best Traditional Romance and has won awards from *Romantic Times BOOKclub* for Best Silhouette Special Edition and Best Silhouette in addition to appearing on the *USA TODAY* bestseller list. Recently resettled in Northern California, Laurie is looking forward to whatever experiences her next novel will send her on.

This story is for Ali, Becka, Susan, Kris and Merry, who wanted to know what happened to the three orphans.

Chapter One

Julianne Martin matched the address on the storefront to the label printed in block letters on the box of pottery she was to deliver. Yes, this was the place.

Something about the building—probably its rundown state—induced a definite sense of caution in her.

This wasn't the most practical part of town to try to sell tourist goods. The Chaco Trading Company out on I-40 was a better location, with plenty of travelers heading west to the Grand Canyon and other national parks, and West Coast residents heading east for family reunions or a tour of the Four Corners and Mesa Verde areas.

Well, it was none of her business. She was just the delivery service…in more ways than one.

She smiled at the thought. As a midwife-nurse-practitioner, she'd been delivering babies on her own for three years. Happy years, she mused in satisfaction, filled with work that she loved.

Two days ago, out near Hosta Butte, she'd helped deliver a darling little boy to a Native American couple. The delighted father had asked her to bring his pottery into town and leave it at this store, which was located on a side street of Gallup, New Mexico. Since she lived only a couple of miles from town, she'd readily agreed.

In this part of the country, with its vast distances people helped each other when they could. Today was Saturday, the first day of October, and the earliest moment she'd had enough free time to keep her promise. She peered in through the open door of the shop.

"Hello?" she called, going inside and pausing while her eyes adjusted to the dim light.

The place was crammed with Indian blankets, baskets and carvings depicting Western themes, all in a helter-skelter fashion. A good dusting and some organization would help sales, in her opinion.

She grinned to herself. Her bossy ways were showing themselves, her brothers would have said. True, she admitted. She liked things to be in good order.

"Whew," she said when she had the heavy box safely on the floor. "Anyone here?"

"Sure."

A man appeared in the doorway behind the cluttered counter. He looked to be close to her own age, which was twenty-six.

No, older, she decided upon inspecting him more closely when he came forward and stopped beside the cash register. He had hair that was almost black and eyes to match. His face was lean and angular. So was his body—tall and wiry and muscular—definitely a man who kept himself in shape. He was perhaps an inch over six feet. He wore faded jeans, a T-shirt with a logo of Ship Rock on it and a billed cap advertising a local bar.

"Can I help you?" he asked, his voice a rich baritone with a gravelly roughness that was oddly pleasing.

His eyes took in everything about her—from her white cotton blouse and khaki cargo shorts to the woven leather huaraches on her feet. He lingered for the briefest second on her legs, which were nicely shaped, if she did say so, then his gaze returned to hers.

The impact of that probing stare did a couple of strange things to her. One, her sense of wariness increased. Two, so did her heartbeat. He made her nervous for no reason that she could pinpoint, but there it was—a hard beating of the heart, tension in every nerve, a quickening deep inside.

Then he smiled.

Awesome was the description that came to mind. His teeth were very white in his tanned face. The smile did nice things for him, relaxing the stern set in the line of his jaw and the frown line between his eyebrows, adding friendly creases at the corners of his eyes.

The dark eyebrows rose slightly in question as he glanced from the box to her.

She stated her business. "I have a box of pottery for you. From Josiah Pareo?" she added when he didn't respond.

"I see."

She sensed something in his tone or a subtle change in manner—she didn't know what, but she felt a sharpening of his attention. Her own sense of caution caused her to quickly survey their surroundings. She saw nothing out of place. When he came around the counter and frowned at the box, she instinctively stepped back.

"Uh, you were expecting the delivery, weren't you?"

"Yeah," he said. "Let's take it to the office. We can inventory it there, then I'll pay you."

She nodded and followed when he lifted the heavy box as if it weighed no more than a pound cake. She glanced at her watch. Past noon. She was tired and ready for a nap since she'd been called out on a delivery at five that morning.

Babies always chose the most inconvenient times

to arrive, but all had gone well with the birth. Now she wanted to go home. Food and sleep. She needed both, she admitted, unable to suppress a huge yawn.

"Have a seat," he said, interrupting the yawn and giving her a speculative once-over.

She wondered what he was speculating about. Maybe her eligibility? She almost grinned at the ridiculous idea. The handsome shopkeeper was all business as he set the box on the floor. Ah, well.

"Sorry, I was up early this morning," she said when he caught her yawning again.

His cocoa-dark eyes slid over her once more, then returned to his task. He opened the cardboard flaps and began placing the pots and vases on a table next to the desk in the messy, crowded office.

Watching his hands, Julianne was reminded of an artist she knew in her hometown of Albuquerque. His fingers were lean, too, the backs of his hands sinewy. Strong hands. Capable. Confident.

This man's were the same. There was also sensitivity in his touch as if he was aware that, in this pottery, he handled the creation of someone's mind and heart. He therefore treated it with great care.

The proprietor's air of concentration surprised her. He examined each piece of pottery as if it were a rare and precious find. There were six pieces in all.

She looked more closely at the wares. They were black glazed, a type that was popular with tourists, with an allover pattern intricately detailed in a way that few potters did nowadays since it was time-consuming.

"How much do you want for these?" he asked.

"I don't know." She'd assumed that was all taken care of. Josiah hadn't mentioned a price. "How much do you think they're worth?"

"A thousand."

At the quick, flat statement, she was totally taken aback. "Really? That seems like a lot. But I actually don't know," she added, not wanting to cast doubts on Josiah's abilities.

She'd had no idea he could get prices like that, especially in a place like this. She glanced around the dusty, cluttered office and shrugged. The tourist trade must be more lucrative than she'd thought.

"Cash or check?" he asked.

She considered. She was pretty sure the couple didn't have a bank account. They'd paid her twenty-five dollars a month for eight months for the delivery of the baby. "Cash."

He counted out ten crisp one hundred-dollar bills and held them out to her. When she reached for the money, his other hand shot out and he snapped a handcuff on her wrist.

She froze in terror. Like images from a horror movie, scenes hurtled through her mind—broken glass from a patio door, a pool of blood, death, the bewilderment of the child who stared at the horrible sight.

In the next instant, the training from years of self-defense courses kicked in, overriding the fear. Instead of struggling to get away, she crashed into the man, using her head to butt him under the chin, since she wasn't tall enough to reach his nose.

She twisted her captured hand, turning his wrist back so he had to let go of the other end of the cuffs. With the heel of her left hand, she slammed into his nose and felt a satisfying crunch of cartilage.

"Ow," he yelled, dropping the cash.

When he tried to recapture her hand, she kicked him in the shin as hard as she could, ignored a sharp pain in her big toe as a result and stomped on his instep as she brought her foot down. *Then* she ran.

Tony Aquilon cursed a blue streak, but that didn't stanch the blood pouring from his nose. Ignoring his wounds—not the least of which was to his pride—he started after her at a dead run. He could hear the fugitive shrieking as she ran down the street.

"Fire!" she shouted. "Fire!"

A mechanic, wiping his hands on a grease rag, appeared at the door of the garage next door. A couple peered out from the used-furniture store across the street. Two beer-drinking, taco-munching patrons at an outside table of a tiny cantina hardly bothered to look up.

Tony grimaced at this new ploy by the damn

sneaky female. He went after her as fast as his limp would allow.

"Call 911," she yelled.

Nobody did anything. Live and Let Live was the motto of the folks in this neighborhood, he could have told her.

"Stop. That's an order," he bellowed, feeling like a fool with his damn nose bleeding all over the place.

She flashed a calculating glance over her shoulder and slowed down a bit.

He caught her halfway down the block just before she scrambled into a car, managing to wedge his arm and body in the opening without getting his fingers or other important parts mangled in the process.

"Got ya," he murmured.

Again she didn't fight fair. Instead of pulling away, she threw herself at him, trying to break his hold.

"Man, you're just full of tricks, aren't you?" he muttered. Holding her was like grasping a maddened wildcat.

While he enjoyed wrestling around with a woman, this wasn't exactly the situation he'd envisioned, he thought with fleeting humor. He had a second to appreciate the strength in her slender curves before she tried to pound his head against the car. He grabbed her hands, spun her around so her back was to him and got her under control. Sort of.

He barely had time to note the tight little butt that

nestled into the groove where his lower body joined his legs before she lifted her arms over her head and tried to choke him with the handcuffs across his throat.

His defensive move was easy due to his much greater upper-body strength. He grabbed her wrists and forced her arms down, trapping her hands across her waist, his arms wrapped around her. Now he simply held her while she squirmed against him like the proverbial worm on a hot rock.

They stayed there panting, their minds busy with plans, hers obviously on escape, his on holding her without further injury to his nose, pride and other vulnerable parts.

"Okay," he said, "I'm going to ease up. No tricks," he warned and stepped away from her, acutely aware of her well-toned body, her feminine shape and her heaving bosom that had lightly touched his upper arm with each breath. He astutely kept her trapped in the triangle of the car, its open door and his body.

She pivoted toward him and tried to poke his eyes out with two fingers.

"That isn't ladylike," he informed her, grabbing the cuffs and managing to get both her hands secured at last.

"Please, call the police," she called to the men at the cantina where the cook had joined the two diners.

"For God's sake," Tony snapped. "I *am* the police."

"You think I'd believe that for a minute?"

He ignored her sarcasm. "You're under arrest."

"What for?"

"Resisting arrest for one. Passing stolen goods for another. Assaulting an officer. Leaving the scene of a crime." He gave her a grin, starting to feel good about the situation now that he had her subdued. Somewhat subdued, he added to himself, wary of another attack from her. "You're good for twenty years to life, honey."

She then gave one of the best performances of shocked outrage he'd ever witnessed. "Resisting…stolen goods…assaulting an officer," she spluttered incredulously. "*You* were the one doing the assaulting. *I* was merely defending myself. Besides, you don't look like any policeman I ever saw."

Using one hand and keeping the other on her, he got out his badge and flipped the cover open.

"Anthony Aquilon, Special Investigator, National Park Service," she read aloud. "We're not in a national park. You don't have the authority to arrest anyone."

"Guess again. Those were very old, very rare Native American artifacts stolen from the new dig site up in Chaco Canyon." He gave her another grin as he put his badge away, then pressed a handkerchief to his nose. Most of the bleeding had stopped in spite of the chase and the fact that adrenaline was kicking through his veins at mach speed.

Using his cell phone, he called in reinforcements in the form of his counterpart with the state cops, Chuck Diaz.

Chuck was one of the good guys. Forty-six. Overweight by fifty pounds. Sneaked smokes when he thought no one was looking. Worried about his wife leaving him and his teenage daughter getting in with the wrong crowd. He was also conscientious about doing his job.

Tony heaved a sigh. With this perp he might need the cavalry to assist in the arrest. Where was John Wayne when a guy needed him?

After making the call, he glanced up and down the street. Now that the threat of danger was past, interested citizens watched the action from every doorway.

Gingerly wiping the remains of the blood on the hankie, he sighed again. It was Saturday. He had a date that night with an attractive woman introduced to him by a friend. He would have to cancel it or else he was going to make a great impression with a swollen nose and blackened eyes.

He tossed a glare at the perp. She tossed it right back.

The sound of sirens interrupted the sensual awareness of the lithe, very feminine body trapped between him and the modest compact vehicle she'd tried to escape in. Warmth radiated from both of them. Sweat dripped from their faces, soaking his T-shirt and her blouse. He kept a hand in the middle of her back in case she pulled a sudden move.

Intensified by their combined heat, his aftershave

mingled with the heady aroma of the floral perfume she wore. The scent filled his nostrils as he took a slow, deep breath. Reinforcements arrived before his senses were completely swamped by images that were definitely not appropriate to the circumstances.

"Thank goodness," his prisoner muttered. "The *real* police. Now we'll get this straightened out."

"Hey, what's happening?" Chuck asked, getting out of the state-supplied SUV after a dramatic halt in front of her car to block any escape attempt.

This time her act was one of self-righteous indignation. "This mule-headed investigator with the park service has gotten things totally confused. He thinks I tried to sell stolen goods. He's wrong, but he won't listen."

Chuck's blue eyes widened in surprise at her heated announcement and turned to him.

Tony shrugged and heaved an exasperated breath. He wouldn't have been surprised if she managed to outfox all of them and take off in the police cruiser. He clamped a hand firmly on her upper arm and shot his partner a questioning glance when two young state patrolmen pulled up behind her vehicle.

"The way it sounded when you called, I thought we could use some backup," Chuck explained. "I, uh, see you have the suspect apprehended, though."

"I am not a suspect! I haven't done anything wrong," she stated with great dignity. "I want to speak to whoever's in charge of this…this person."

Tony ignored the diatribe, sucked in another breath and backed away slowly, never relaxing his vigil for an instant. "Watch it," he said. "She's deadly."

The cops looked him and the prisoner over.

"Yeah. Deadly," Chuck agreed with a suppressed chortle.

While the two state cops remained to guard the store, Julianne was informed of her Miranda rights, put in the back of the cruiser and taken to the nearest state police office. No one paid the slightest attention to her protests.

"Save it for the judge," her captor told her.

She was led inside the squat concrete block structure, still handcuffed like some kind of dangerous lunatic. She couldn't believe she was under arrest for doing a favor for someone.

A tiny trickle of fright shivered along her spine as she stood inside the cool lobby of the building. She quickly suppressed it. As soon as Josiah came and verified her story, all would be resolved and she could go home.

Another thought came to her. She probably should inform the tribal chairman of her predicament. "I need to call my boss," she informed the National Park detective, who kept a hand on her arm.

"In a minute," he told her.

She first had to answer a lot of questions about

herself—name, age, date of birth, address, occupation—then be fingerprinted like a common thief. She just barely held her indignation in check.

"This is stupid," she said to the handsome bully who'd arrested her and who was apparently well-known to the local officials.

Aquilon. The name was familiar, but she couldn't say why. The other police officers acted as if he had done something heroic. Their glances at her were sort of smirky, she thought.

"It's all a mistake," she added.

"That's what they all say, kid." The detail sergeant handed her a paper towel to wipe her fingers. He was also in charge of evidence. He inventoried the box of pots, numbered it and gave the arresting detective a receipt. He bagged her purse, watch and sterling silver earrings and handed the receipt to her.

"Good job," he said to Aquilon, much to Julianne's dismay.

The sergeant led the way down a short hallway and into an interrogation room. She'd been in one of these before but for pro bono work in dealing with a young culprit who'd stolen food for his sick mother. As the home-health nurse on the case, she'd testified in his defense.

"The charges will be dropped as soon as my boss gets here," she informed her captor, who leaned against the door frame and observed her with no expression in his dark eyes. Unease flittered through her again. There was no way those silly charges would stick, she assured her sinking spirits, not for doing a good deed. She needed only to remain calm until the situation was cleared up.

"Who's your boss?" the superhero asked.

"Chief Windover. He can vouch for me. He's head of the tribal council. I have a contract to provide health services for the people," she explained, using the name the tribe preferred in referring to themselves. She sat at the table and scrubbed at the black residue on her fingers.

"Are you Hopi?" Aquilon demanded. He and the desk sergeant exchanged glances.

She realized if she answered in the affirmative she would probably be turned over to the tribe for them to deal with the crime. However, while she was one-eighth Native American on her maternal side, she didn't belong to the local tribe.

"No, but as a nurse-midwife, I do prenatal and delivery care for the tribe. I also run a clinic three days a week and do home visits in special cases."

After her explanation, the sergeant nodded to the investigator and left the room. The inquisition continued.

"Why were you transporting and selling artifacts?"

"I wasn't. Those were Josiah's pots, not artifacts."

"Guess again. All six are priceless antiques stolen from the new dig down in the canyon."

"Chaco Canyon, yes, you said that earlier. But I'm sure you're mistaken. Josiah wouldn't—"

"What was your cut?" he demanded, startling her by suddenly leaning across the table and getting right in her face while he gave her a really mean stare.

"Nothing. Didn't you hear me? This is some kind of misunderstanding. Those pots aren't priceless." She tossed the paper towel on the table and crossed her arms. "Get an expert in here. Dr. Jones from the museum will set you straight."

The older detective came in. He set a cup of coffee in front of her and kept one for himself. "Here. Sorry, we're out of cream and sugar."

"Thank you." She took a sip of the coffee that tasted as if it had been made a week ago and left on the burner ever since. Nonetheless, she didn't complain.

"Tony, here, is an expert on Native American art, including the ancient stuff," the older man continued, pulling up a chair and sitting across from her.

"Him?" she said skeptically.

"That's right," the man called Chuck assured her. "He's practically a professor."

They both looked at the younger man, who leaned against the dingy wall. "Not quite," he said with an irritated glance at the other man, as if Chuck had given away secrets he didn't want to share. "I still have the dissertation to complete."

"For your Ph.D.?" she questioned in open disbelief.

"Yeah." His steady stare dared her to make something of it.

"I'm impressed," she said, but with a sardonic edge she couldn't quite conceal.

She tried to picture him as a staid professor of antiquities. The image was too stiff and formal to associate with the dynamic man who'd wrestled with her, arrested her and now observed her in an impassive manner as if her protests of innocence made no impression on him at all.

Tony Aquilon. Where had she heard the name?

She sighed. "I don't know anything about ancient artifacts or any finds in Chaco Canyon or anywhere else. The couple needed money and asked me to take the pots to town. I said I would since they live over an hour from here and had just had their first child. He needed to stay with the mother and baby. It was the cutest little boy—"

A snort from the younger detective cut her off.

Okay, so she did love babies and tended to go on and on about them. But they were so sweet and trusting, something she hadn't been in a long time.

Not since she was ten years old.

At that time two men had broken into her home and raped and killed her mom. She'd come home from school and found the horrible crime scene. Since that day, her father had made sure she and her two brothers learned self-defense, sending them to more advanced courses each year until they'd passed them all. Lots of noise and surprise tactics were the keys to escaping an enemy.

Her training hadn't stopped her captor from arresting her, though. Recalling the strength in his embrace as he'd locked her in his arms, she was somewhat stunned as she realized he'd been incredibly gentle with her, not hurting her at all during the struggle.

She examined her wrist. Not a mark on it, not even a bruise from the handcuffs. Studying the special investigator covertly, she had to admit he was an enigma—a man who applied his strength with care instead of brute force.

"If you're innocent, why did you run?" the special investigator demanded. He gingerly felt his nose.

"Because that's what a normal person does when a stranger tries to nab you," she informed him. "You need to put ice on that. It'll stop the swelling."

He gave her a narrow look, considered, then headed out of the room. "I should take a bath in the damn stuff," she heard him mutter just before the door closed behind him.

"I think you bruised his pride," the older detective said in a kind manner. "Who was it you said we should call?"

"Chief Windover. I have a number for him." She gave the man the information. Once they checked her credentials, they would realize they had made a mistake and she would be free to go home.

The older man nodded. "Okay. I'll see if we can't get this straightened out."

After he left, Julianne slumped into the chair. While she hadn't been injured, she felt sore and just plain beat. Well, no wonder, after all that running and then wrestling around with the superhero.

Okay, so he was a special investigator with the National Park Service and the other cops obviously knew and respected him. That he was also an expert on ancient artifacts and a hunk was rather intriguing.

So?

So she didn't know, except he made her feel…funny. Studying her wrist, she conceded he'd used no more force than necessary to subdue her, while she'd used every evasive maneuver she knew.

"Ohh," she groaned, recalling all she'd done to get away. The judge would probably lock her up forever for breaking his nose.

Which he deserved for scaring the devil out of her by yanking out those handcuffs and trying to clamp them on her without warning. If he'd explained himself, then she could have explained her part in the supposed crime and all would have been resolved.

She was still frowning when he returned, holding an ice pack to his nose. Seeing it made her feel somewhat guilty for being the cause. But only a little bit, she added, since it was his fault in the first place.

"Chief Windover is gone for the weekend," he said.

"Oh, that's right. He's taken his family camping and fishing at Many Farms Lake." She snapped her fingers. "That's where I heard of you."

"I haven't been to Many Farms Lake, wherever that is."

"Arizona, near Canyon De Chelly. However, it was while I was in the chief's office that I heard of you. He got a call from the park service. Your name was mentioned. He said he would alert the tribal police. I assumed you were an escaped convict."

"I let the authorities know I was investigating a case and would be on the reservation at times. I needed a counterpart with their law enforcement department to work with me."

"Like Officer Diaz with the state police here?"

"Yeah, like Chuck."

"Well, that explains everything," she said, standing. "I'm glad we had this chat. Now I need to get home and—"

"You're not going anywhere," he informed her.

She tried for calm. "Now that you know who I am and that I'm not guilty of anything, aren't you going to let me go?"

"No way."

"Why not?" It came out a belligerent snarl.

"Until we contact the chief, we have no one to vouch for you."

"That is the stupidest thing I ever heard. You have my driver's license and address. You can call anyone on the council or one of the clinical staff. Surely that's enough to check out my identity."

"Maybe, but the law doesn't work that way. Your

being a nurse doesn't mean anything. There are serious charges against you. Transporting stolen goods for one. Selling priceless artifacts, for another. You also resisted arrest, which I could have added to the list but didn't," he stated as if he'd done her a huge favor, his thick eyebrows drawn into a severe frown above the ice bag.

"If you'd shown me your badge first and told me what was happening, we could have talked it over without all that, uh, hassle."

"Hassle?" he said. "You bruised my nose and stomped my foot. That was just the beginning. Once I caught you, you tried to choke me with the cuffs, not to mention the attempt to poke me in the eyes. Hassle? It was assault and battery in my book." He waved an arm expansively.

"That was self-defense," she told him hotly. "It's very frightening to a woman to be grabbed by a strange man. Keep that ice pack on your nose."

He clamped the bag back on his face and winced in pain. "Anyway," he continued, "you'll have to stay here until we can check out your story."

"Here, as in jail?"

"Yeah."

She couldn't believe this. It was just too, too absurd for words. It belatedly occurred to her that she might actually need some professional help. "I want to call my brother. He's an attorney. He'll tell you who I am."

"You'll have to ask the D.A. if you can have another call." He started for the door.

"I haven't had the first one yet."

"Chief Windover. That was who you asked for."

"I demand to see somebody. Where is this district attorney?"

He shrugged. "The office is closed for the weekend. You'll have to wait until Monday to talk to him. Also," he added when she started to protest, "the courthouse is closed, too. There's no judge to listen to your case and set bail. Not that I would recommend bail. You're a prime candidate to flee, in my opinion."

"Which you would just have to give, wouldn't you?"

His smile was barely visible under the ice pack. "It would be my civic duty."

With that, he left her alone in the narrow ugly room with its scarred table and three chairs, one of which had a broken leg. The anger, sarcasm and just plain disbelief faded. She blinked back unexpected tears, feeling as abandoned as a two-year-old lost in a department store.

Not that she considered *him* a savior. The handsome, albeit unreasonable, detective was the one who'd gotten her into this mess. Well, Josiah, too. She had a thing or two to say to that innocent-acting young man.

The grizzled sergeant stuck his head in the door. "Let's go," he said.

"Am I free?" she asked in surprised relief.

He gave her a look that said she wasn't.

"What about my car? It isn't locked. Someone could steal it."

"After it was searched, it was towed in."

"Searched? Towed?" she repeated indignantly.

The officer wouldn't be drawn into further conversation. He shrugged off her questions, took her to a cell and locked the door after she was inside.

She was a prisoner.

Chapter Two

After canceling his date, Tony drove home, staring at the road while the late-afternoon sun began its glide into the evening. He examined the swelling across his nose and under his eyes. On the way to his temporary home, a room in the local park head-quarters barracks, his thoughts strayed to the jail. He wondered what the captive was doing at this moment. Probably giving an earful to whoever happened to be handy about her wrongful arrest.

She'd probably sue him if she was innocent.

At the long, low residence barracks, he parked in front of his unit, which was one big room with a bed, sitting area and kitchen consisting of an under-the-counter fridge, a two-burner hot plate, a sink and a microwave, and went inside. He had his own bathroom here, unlike some hostels he'd stayed at during his college years while working for the park service.

All the comforts of home.

The nosebleed returned when he took a shower. Ten minutes later, dressed in jeans and a sweatshirt, he held a new batch of ice cubes to his nose while he studied the contents of the cabinets.

As usual, his choices ran to cereal, sandwiches or soup. Not exactly a gourmet selection, but better than the food the suspect would likely get in jail.

He suddenly wished he could confide the happenings of the day to his foster uncle. Jefferson Aquilon—his mom had once been married to Uncle Jeff's brother, so the older man was sort of a stepuncle—had always treated him and his sister, Krista, as if they were his own flesh and blood, the same as Jeremy, a nephew who was also an orphan and their stepcousin. Uncle Jeff was a good listener.

Tony needed some advice on his own confusing reactions to the suspect. The fact that he halfway believed her story probably meant he was ready for the loony bin.

Strangest of all, he regretted that she would have to spend the weekend in jail and wondered if he should call the D.A. and judge at home to see what they thought should be done with her.

Man, what was he thinking? After what she did to him, she didn't deserve any special treatment. No way.

He selected a can of soup and made a ham sandwich, then settled in front of the television to catch the news while he ate the solitary meal. With the summer help gone from the barracks and the information office closed, he had the place to himself.

The world news didn't distract his thoughts from the prisoner, he found. It was probably scary to be locked in jail. Especially if she was as innocent as she proclaimed.

Not that he was considering taking her side. He wasn't that gullible to her charms, although she'd felt pretty good nestled against him. As if she belonged there.

Shaking his head at the fantasy, he finished the meal and cut a huge slice from a chocolate cake he'd bought at the grocery that morning. It seemed an age since he'd blithely gotten up, done the shopping and gone down to open the souvenir store at nine o'clock.

And arrested one of the most fascinating suspects he'd ever met after a tussle that lingered in his mind with as much stubborn determination as she'd displayed in her attempts to escape.

Taking the last bite of cake, he savored the chocolate flavor, then wondered if prisoners got dessert.

Twenty minutes later, after a change of clothing, Tony pulled up in front of the state patrol building. He was still arguing with himself about the wisdom of being here when he went inside. He'd decided to use the treat to soften up the suspect and get some info out of her about her contacts with the gang of thieves looting the Chaco sites, assuming there was a gang and the thefts over the past year were related.

"I, uh, brought the nurse something," he said to the sergeant at the desk. It wasn't the same one as earlier in the day.

"What nurse?"

"The suspect I brought in this afternoon. I figured she might need some nourishment after having dinner in here."

"Hey, we have the meals catered," the night-duty officer declared.

"Yeah, right."

After a chuckle, the man said, "I'll have to check what's in the bag."

Tony waited, feeling more and more foolish as the cop opened the bag, examined a plastic fork, then the napkin and removed the top from the plastic bowl. "Man, that looks good," he said.

"Sorry, I didn't bring any extra," Tony told the sarge with a sardonic smile. "Got any fresh coffee?"

"Yeah, I made a pot when I came on duty less than an hour ago. Want me to bring you some?"

"That would be great."

The officer repacked the treat. "I'll buzz you in. She's in cell number one."

* * *

The television set mounted on the wall outside the cell was turned on, but Julianne wasn't listening to the news. She was still wound up from the ordeal with the police.

In spite of being dead tired, she couldn't get into the mood to sleep. If she'd been at home, she would have tried aromatherapy. Lavender was supposed to be soothing when steeped in hot water. Chamomile tea was a sleep aid, but she doubted the jailer had any on hand.

A loud buzz startled her. The door to the cell block opened and a man walked in. Her heart knotted up in alarm, then relaxed as she realized who he was.

"Oh, for heaven's sake," she muttered. She rose from the hard bunk. Glaring between the bars on the door, she demanded, "What are you doing here?"

Her nemesis from the tourist shop stopped in front of her. "I brought you a present."

He held out a brown paper bag. She eyed it as if it might explode any second.

"It's okay," he assured her. "It's cake."

"Cake," she repeated suspiciously.

He gave her a quick but thorough perusal as he slipped the bag between the bars. "It's safe," he added with an ironic grin before grimacing and touching his swollen nose.

Twin bruises under his eyes gave him the masked

look of a raccoon. She frowned at the pang of guilt that assailed her and reminded herself she'd acted in self-defense.

"Look," he said, "I felt kind of bad about the hassle we had earlier, I thought about the jail food, so I, uh, brought you some dessert. Chocolate cake."

She took the treat and sat on the cot. "You're weird," she told him. "I know it's a slow night since there's no one else in jail, but I'd have thought you could find something more interesting to do on a Saturday evening than hang out at the jail."

He snorted. "You're in the women's cell block. There are several inmates in the men's section." He glanced at the two empty cells. "I guess they don't get many woman criminals around here."

She ignored the anger that demanded she refute his calling her a criminal. Instead, she gave him a fulminating glance, then opened the brown bag and removed the container.

The fury receded somewhat when she saw the contents. Chocolate was one of her favorite things. She wisely decided not to throw the cake in his face.

When the night-duty officer brought in two cups of coffee, she accepted one of those, too, and thanked the man. Taking a bite of the dessert, she closed her eyes, savoring the rich flavor.

"I have a question," her captor said, pulling a chair closer to the bars and taking a seat. "Who taught you how to take defensive action?"

For a second she remembered being ten and coming home from school, excited because she'd gotten a perfect score on her math test, then going into the house and finding her mother.

It wasn't until she'd been in nurses' training and a rape victim had been brought into the emergency room during her rotation there that she'd realized what her mother must have gone through that terrible afternoon.

Julianne locked the memory away as ancient pain careened around her chest, but it was still a moment before she could speak. "My father sent me and my two brothers to self-defense classes while we were growing up."

She could almost see the wheels turning in his head as he considered the information. Earlier in the day, when she'd given her personal information, she'd reported her father as her next of kin and her mother as deceased.

"Was there any particular reason he thought you needed them?" he asked.

Replacing the bowl and fork in the bag, she faced him without allowing any expression in her tone. "Our home was broken into when I was ten. My mother was killed."

For a second his face took on the fierce expression of a warrior who would defend his tribe to his last breath, then it softened and she recognized other emotions—a certain kindness for those who'd been hurt, a touch of sympathy, maybe pity.

Pity was something she didn't want and didn't know how to handle when it was offered. She usually mumbled something about life going on and changed the subject, but now her throat closed and she couldn't say a word. Old emotions, heightened by the events of the day, threatened to overcome her. She swallowed hard and refused to give in to them.

"Were you there when it happened?"

She shook her head.

"Did they find whoever did it?"

Again she indicated the negative.

"Crimes by total strangers are not often solved," he told her, his tone gentle as if she were still that hurt child of long ago. "There's no connection or motive for police to follow as there is with husbands or boyfriends."

"Yes, that's what the detective said who handled the case." She returned the bag to him, having eaten three or four bites of the treat. She took a drink of coffee and noted that it was much better than the brew Chuck had given her earlier. The warmth eased the cold spot in her chest, and she relaxed once more. "Thank you for the cake. That was thoughtful. Now I have a question. Why did you bring it?"

"Well," he drawled, "I know that jail food comes from the lowest bidder."

That made her laugh. "It wasn't so bad. We had

spaghetti and rolls and a piece of lettuce with a sliver of carrot that was supposed to be a salad, I think."

After that they talked about the worst meals they'd ever had as if they were acquaintances who were fast becoming friends. He told her the three kids in his family had to take turns preparing meals once a week. He had her cracking up over his description of recipes made with green stuff like lime gelatin or broccoli. His cousin Jeremy would clutch his throat and accuse him of trying to poison them.

"Your family sounds like mine," she told him. "I took nutrition classes in college, but I could never convince my brothers that green, leafy vegetables were really good for them. They now send me magazine clippings that extol the value of blueberries."

"Ah, smart men," he said.

Laughing, she glanced at him, then away. Then, pulled by unexpected forces stronger than her will, she met his gaze through the dull glint of the steel bars. Their eyes locked. The laughter faded.

Something was happening to her. She felt it as a primal shift somewhere in her soul. He felt it, too, she thought. His chest lifted and fell in a slow, careful breath as if he, too, were on shaky ground.

She looked away, wondering how they could have gone from laughter to something profound and infinitely challenging in a heartbeat.

Maybe arresting people did that, although it wasn't what she would call a bonding event. Recalling his arousal as they struggled, she felt heat creep up her neck. *That* had certainly been a new and different experience for her.

He could have hurt her, but he hadn't. Instead of fury, she'd seen self-mocking humor in his eyes when he'd told her to quit thrashing about.

Though she'd been frightened until he'd shown her his badge, their struggle had been oddly exciting, too, she decided after she thought it over while sitting here in the cell. Other than her father and brothers, she knew she had a problem with trust of the male half of the population.

The fact was that men always expected more than she was willing to give at the moment. Just when she was starting to feel comfortable with the guy and with kisses and caresses, then, well, things moved too fast, becoming too demanding. One date had accused her of holding out.

She'd been left feeling humiliated and in the wrong for reasons she didn't know. It certainly hadn't increased her comfort level with the opposite sex.

Glancing at her captor's hands as he linked them together between his knees, his gaze on the floor as if deep in thought, she realized that no matter what defensive move she'd made, he'd countered with only enough force to halt it, but not once had he bruised her in any way.

When he'd folded her into his arms and pulled her against him, it was as if she'd been wrapped in a protective cocoon and all he'd wanted to do was keep her from getting hurt. It was such an odd thought....

Staring at the dull green wall, she admitted she was mystified by his visit, by their shared laughter, by the intriguing currents that ran between them that were almost as disturbing as her arrest.

"It's late," he said. "I should leave and let you get some rest."

"I don't think I'll sleep very much tonight."

He nodded. "I was still wound up after the day's excitement, too."

"I'd have thought arresting people was old hat to a special investigator for the National Park Service." Her tone was mildly sarcastic.

He grinned, then winced and touched his nose. She was at once sorry she'd been so rough, even though it was his fault for scaring her.

"Hardly," he said. "Mostly I authenticate archeological finds for the department and set up security, especially on ancient sites like the dig up at the canyon. I investigate thefts and other problems at various national parks. They send me wherever they need some help."

"I see."

Regaining her equilibrium, she decided his work sounded like an easy job to her, nothing that called for springing handcuffs on innocent people without warning.

Gazing at his nose, which was noticeably swollen, she forgot her indignation over the arrest and advised, "You should ice your bruises for forty-eight hours, then switch to four minutes of heat followed by one minute of ice three or four times a day after that for two or three days."

"I kept an ice pack on it most of the afternoon."

"Good." After observing him for a moment when he made no move to leave, she asked quietly, seriously, "What are you really doing here? I think you came because you want something from me."

Before answering, he drank the last of the coffee. He crushed the paper cup and tossed it in a wastebasket near the door, then studied her for several seconds. "I want you to take me to the guy you said gave you the pottery."

"Tonight?" she asked incredulously as disappointment hit her. She realized the cake, the kindness and the easy laughter had been a method of softening her up before he made the request.

"No, but soon. I don't want him to get word that something funny went on at the store."

Leaning against the wall behind the cot, she took a drink of coffee and noticed he was dressed in dark slacks, a white shirt informally open at the neck and well-shined loafers. She'd already noticed his aftershave, the fragrance familiar to her from their earlier encounter.

So, he'd cleaned up before coming to the jail. Was that part of the ploy to win her confidence and encourage a sense of camaraderie between them?

Tired and discouraged, she regretted letting herself drift into familiarity, especially the sharing of her past. It was something she rarely talked about, but he'd seemed truly concerned, as if he already knew that she'd been injured by events of long ago.

"How far is his place from town?" he continued.

"Over fifty miles, off Standing Rock Road."

"I'll be here around eight in the morning to pick you up."

"Will they let me out of jail?"

"You'll be released into my custody." His tone implied it would be no problem.

"If we find Josiah and he confirms my story, will I then be free?"

He hesitated, then said, "I'll talk to the district attorney on your behalf. He's the one who'll decide whether to charge you with a crime or let you off if you cooperate."

"I'll cooperate," she assured him coldly. "I want to clear my name as soon as possible and put this experience behind me."

And you, she added silently. She wanted him out of her life. He was a threat, although she couldn't say how.

When he rose, she, too, stood. He rattled the doorknob, the buzzer sounded and he walked out, leaving her standing behind the metal bars of the tiny cell. She immediately experienced the sense of abandonment again, as if he was her only savior in a world she no longer knew.

She rubbed her wrists, but there were no purple marks from fingers digging too harshly into her flesh. She remembered how careful he'd been when examining the priceless pottery and the way he'd stared into her eyes as if looking directly into her soul. She'd never felt that before. For the briefest moment, she wondered what it would be like to have him wrap her in his arms again, to feel his lips on hers…

She blinked, appalled at the strange path her mind had taken. Pressing her hands against her eyes, she felt dismay, anger, exasperation and other feelings too tangled to comprehend.

Glancing around the cell, she made up her mind to fight fire with fire. She had to smile. She knew just who she needed to get in touch with. Special Investigator Aquilon might be a force to be reckoned with, but she wasn't without resources of her own.

"Sergeant," she yelled. "Sergeant, I need to talk to you."

Chapter Three

Tony hit the snooze alarm twice before he could drag himself out of bed and into Sunday morning. After washing up and dressing, he wandered into the kitchen and poured a cup of fresh coffee, which was ready thanks to the modern marvel of a timer on the coffeemaker.

What the heck was he doing up at six-thirty when this was the one day of the week he could catch up on his sleep?

Oh, yeah, the prisoner. He had work to do today.

He thought about going over and taking her to breakfast before they went searching for the man who gave her the pottery to deliver. If there was such a person, he added, frowning at his tendency to believe her story without any corroborating evidence.

Except for the earnestness of her gaze when she'd looked him directly in the eye. And the set of her mouth, which turned up at the corners in the most alluring way, when she'd stated she wanted to clear her name.

He groaned under his breath as his body went into full alert. Last night his dreams had been so hot it was a wonder the bed hadn't caught fire. Without having to think about crimes and arrests, his subconscious had been free to consider other delightful things a man and woman could do when they were in such close proximity.

A cold—very cold—shower helped get things calmed down. After a quick breakfast, he headed for the station house. While she was technically his prisoner, there were papers to fill out before he could whisk her out of jail.

One of the problems with his line of work was jurisdiction. When it came to ancient artifacts, who was the authority—the park service? The tribal police? The local state and/or county officials? It was always a pain to sort through and often only a very fine, blurry line separated the legal powers. In this case, because Chuck had been in on the arrest and the Hopi claimed all artifacts as part of their culture, it made the question even more contentious.

However, he'd found he could usually work through the system with a little diplomacy. Since Julianne was cooperating, he didn't see any reason to keep her in jail.

Neither did a lot of other people.

Bedlam reigned when he arrived at the state police headquarters. He had to push his way through a mob to get to the desk.

"What's going on?" he asked the detail sergeant from the previous day when he and Chuck had brought in the suspect. At that moment he noticed Julianne standing to one side, her purse in her hand. "Who let her out?" he demanded. "Who authorized it?"

"The county judge," the sarge replied. "Apparently her brother called the chief of the tribal council. The chief called the tribal attorney, who called the county judge. The judge's assistant came in with a release order this morning, along with about fifty members of the Native American Women's Advisory Council and one of the tribal elders. She posted bail, so she's free."

Tony turned to Julianne, whose innocent smile would have melted the heart of an iceberg.

"How did your brother get word?" he asked, giving her a narrow-eyed scowl.

"Last night after you left, the sergeant let me use my cell phone to call him…after I explained the governor would hear about my arrest and false imprisonment as soon as Chief Windover returned."

The tribal elder, wearing a traditional Hopi braid and two eagle feathers, stepped forward. He looked old enough and wizened enough to be an artifact from the dig.

"The tribe has jurisdiction in the case," he informed Tony. "The council had an emergency meeting last night and decided Julianne was to be freed."

"Well," Julianne said. "I'm ready to go. Since I have my car, I can lead you to the spot, then return home while you arrest everybody," she said brightly.

"You'll ride with me." It was time for him to take charge. "I have authority in this case," he told the elder and the two older women lined up beside him. "I was planning on releasing her this morning. She's cooperating in the investigation."

"Of course she is," one of the women said. "She's a wonderful person. She saved my grandson's life when he stopped breathing shortly after he was born." Her glare dared him to contradict her statement.

He sighed and turned to the desk sergeant. "Give me the custody papers. I'm taking charge of her." He doggedly filled out the papers in spite of protests from the NAWAC. "She'll be free to go home as long as she doesn't leave the state," he told them.

"It's okay," Julianne spoke up when the women looked as if they might attack. "He and I are working together on this. Thank you so much for coming down and helping me out. I really appreciate it."

Tony watched as she hugged the elder and his two

primary sidekicks. After promising to kick butt if there was more trouble, the elder and the NAWAC departed.

"Are you ready?" he asked sardonically.

"Yes. Is it okay if I drop my car at my house?"

He nodded, feeling very gracious considering she was in his custody and had nearly gotten him staked out on an anthill by her defenders. He followed her out of town and onto Highway 666, which was where her house was located.

Hmm, 666. Wasn't that the symbol of the devil?

Yeah, and it suited her to a tee.

He would have laughed but it hurt his nose to move his facial muscles that much.

Outside, Julianne flinched at the brightness of the sun on the eastern horizon. She was aware of the park service vehicle that stayed on her tail as she drove out of town.

Two miles up the highway, she turned into the driveway of an adobe two-bedroom cottage that was part of her work compensation. She was thinking of buying it if the council extended her contract. She parked under the lean-to carport and hopped out.

The morning air was like a magic elixir as she inhaled deeply. Freedom. She'd never take it for granted again. Although she felt like laughing and running before the breeze like a bird, she approached the SUV sedately. "Would you mind if I showered and changed clothes before we left?"

The chill of the night lingered on the desert. She rubbed the goose bumps from her arms while she waited for his decision. "I'll make you breakfast," she added when he didn't answer right away.

"I've eaten. But I could use a cup of coffee while I wait."

Her eyes widened with pleasure when she realized he'd given his approval. "Sure. Coming right up." She rushed to the front door. "Uh, you can come in."

After putting on a pot of coffee and showing him where the cups were, she dashed into her bedroom and closed the door. She took the fastest shower in history and returned to the kitchen in fresh slacks and a tank top with a matching overshirt. He stood at the back door that opened onto a covered patio and drank from a coffee mug, his eyes on the arroyo, dry now because there'd been no rain in over two weeks, that wended its way along the edge of the property.

"I'm ready to go, Special Investigator Aquilon," she said, smiling.

He gave her a wary glance. "My name's Anthony. Everyone calls me Tony."

"I'm Julianne, Jules, rhymes with mules, to my smart-mouth brothers." She hadn't a clue as to why she'd added this bit of family information.

"One of those smart-mouth brothers got you out of jail."

"Calhoon," she told him. "Cal's the oldest, I'm

the middle and Sam's the youngest in our family. Dad used to tease the boys, saying we three kids were like an Oreo and I was the sweet in the middle."

Her guest carefully touched his nose, which she thought looked much better, hardly any swelling at all. "Yeah," he said, "real sweet."

When she laughed, he shook his head, but the corners of his mouth turned up a bit.

"Where does your family live?" he asked.

"Albuquerque, which is where I was born and raised. My brothers live there, too." She filled a travel mug with coffee. "Well, I'm ready for the great adventure."

He looked heavenward as if asking for patience.

"I've never arrested anyone before," she explained.

"You're not now. I'm the arresting officer."

"Whatever," she said blithely. Nothing could ruin her exuberance at being out of jail.

He led the way to the SUV and saw her inside before climbing in the driver's side. "Which way?"

"North." She watched his hands as he put the truck in gear and backed out.

She'd thought of him last night before she fell asleep, of the strength in his hands and how his body had felt against hers, pinning her in place against the dusty car. The long, hard ridge in his jeans had been unmistakable.

Like yesterday, a strange clamoring rose in her, as if a dormant part of her had awakened and demanded attention. She'd always been cautious, though, so this internal heat was surprising.

After they were on their way, she asked, "Are you still pressing charges against me? I was told I would have to report to a judge for a hearing."

He flicked her a probing glance. The man had a way of looking a person over as if he could dig out the truth no matter how much she tried to hide it.

"If your alibi holds up, then we'll see," he said.

"What alibi?"

"If Josiah Pareo confirms your story, then the onus will be on him to come up with a good explanation for having those artifacts."

"He will," she said. "He and his wife. They were a nice young couple, very concerned about their new baby and its welfare. I'm sure he'll straighten this out."

"Hmm," the special investigator said.

It was a cop's duty to be skeptical, so she decided to forgive him for his doubts.

"How far up this way?" he asked, once they were on the highway heading toward Ship Rock.

"Take a right when you get to the Coyote Canyon Road. Go almost to the turnoff to Standing Rock. Turn left—"

"Okay, alert me when we get to the left turn," he interrupted, a frown line creasing his forehead.

She missed his smile, she realized, as he reverted to the stern investigator of yesterday. Yesterday! Less than twenty-four hours, yet she felt as if she'd lived an eon since then. Studying his handsome profile, it seemed odd that she'd only just met this man.

"What's funny?" he asked.

"I was wondering if we'd met in another life. You seem awfully familiar."

"Yeah, right."

She laughed at his sardonic tone, then concentrated on the road so she wouldn't miss the dirt track to the couple's trailer after he made the correct right turn. "It's coming up. Here. Turn left here."

He made the turn. A dust trail rose behind them. It was slow going for the next two miles due to the ruts. They rounded the last curve. The coyote fence was there, but the yard was empty.

"It's gone," she said. "The trailer is gone."

Julianne went inside the gate, which had been left open, and walked around the rectangle of yard. A dry creek bed and two rows of stacked rocks indicated where the house trailer had once stood. Faint traces of wavy lines were barely visible in the gritty dirt.

"He used a piece of brush to mark out the tire treads," Tony told her, squatting on his haunches to study the ground.

"Why?"

"To cover his tracks."

She shook her head in disbelief as she stared at the ground where once a home had been. "I was here two days ago. No, three. The baby was born on

Thursday. I filled out the papers and did the baby's footprints for the birth certificate so I could file it with the tribal records office."

"Well, they're gone now. Someone must have gotten word to them that there was a sting operation going down. Did you get prints on the parents?"

She nodded. "The tribe has us do thumbprints." Her eyes widened as she realized the implication of his words. "The shop was a fake?"

"A front," he corrected. "We set it up and let it be known we wanted Indian goods. Good Indian goods," he added with a significant glance at her.

"The pottery," she murmured, disappointed in the couple who'd certainly played her for a fool. "I can't believe they stole those things."

"Believe it," he said. "What about the prints? Did you keep a record of them?"

"No. You can get a copy from the tribal office."

"Fine."

She observed while he looked over the site.

A large section of coyote fence, which was made from the canes of the infamous ocotillo nailed side by side onto wooden supports, had been loosened and pulled aside in order to drive the trailer through to the dirt lane.

The tracks were brushed out on that side of the fence, too. She recalled something. "He drove a blue pickup," she told the special investigator. She described the make and model and a dent in one fender.

"What else do you remember about them?"

"Well, they were young, both twenty-one. They belonged to the Hopi. He was a mechanic."

"Ah," the detective said.

"Ah, what?"

"Did he work at the garage near the shop?"

"I don't know."

His eyes narrowed. "Maybe the mechanic who watched the big chase scene alerted him to the bust. I'll check on that tomorrow." He made a note in a little spiral pad, then searched around once more. "There's nothing here, not even a trash pile," he finally concluded.

"You're very thorough."

Those dark eyes cut to her like the flick of a whip on bare skin. "That's my job," he stated, and headed for his vehicle. He didn't seem to think she was much help.

She trailed behind him.

"What's wrong?" he asked when they were on the road.

"I'm worried about them and the baby." She sighed. "Life can be so hard. They don't have much money. Probably someone promised them a large cut of the profits if they would sell the artifacts. They didn't mean any harm."

"Yeah, they were innocents."

She sighed again. "I don't think that. Every population has its share of good people and bad. The couple must have desperately needed money, though." She studied him. "You know a lot about artifacts. Is your interest because you have Native American ancestry?"

He nodded. "My great-grandmother was Sioux."

"I see."

"You got time to go out to the dig?" he asked, stopping at the county road.

She was surprised by the invitation. "Yes. It sounds very interesting."

"I'd planned on coming out and checking over the security at the site this morning. Since we're this close, it would be simpler to go there now."

He turned left instead of right and headed past the rock formation that gave the area its name. There were two Chaco culture sites, he told her. He took the road to the second one, which was farther north from where they were.

"Have you been here?" he asked as they neared Pueblo Bonito.

"Once, a long time ago with my father and brothers. I loved exploring the village. It reminds me that people haven't changed that much in hundreds or thousands of years. They needed shelter and ways to make a living in order to provide food and clothing for their families back then just as we do today."

"And they built apartment buildings and lived in towns, too," he added, driving down a road that was

off-limits except for park service personnel. "Like
the Roman roads, theirs were built to last."

"Yes," she agreed. When they arrived at the main
ruins, she murmured in awe of the multistory dwellings that backed up to a sandstone cliff, and tried to
recall all she'd read about the people who built them.
"I've forgotten when this area was occupied."

"The Chaco culture flourished from around 850
to 1250 A.D.," he told her. "We know of at least
thirteen major pueblos. This one, Pueblo Bonito,
was one of the leading pre-Columbian villages
outside Mexico. It was a hub of commerce, admin-
istration and ceremony. See the great house?"

She peered in the direction he pointed as he drove
slowly along the canyon. "Yes."

"It's four or five stories high and has over six
hundred rooms and forty kivas, which were ceremonial chambers. The whole settlement was planned
and executed in stages. Can you imagine the knowledge in engineering, architecture and masonry
required for such an undertaking?"

"All without powered tools," she added.

"Yes."

"What happened to the people who lived here?"

"They're still around. The Pueblos and Hopi have
oral histories of migrations from this area. The
Navajo, although they aren't considered Puebloan,
also trace some of their clans back to Chaco."

Julianne stared at the ruins and imagined the

bustling community going about its daily business. Although the park wasn't crowded, she noticed two groups of people being led through the stone rooms by park rangers. One of the rangers spotted them and waved. Tony waved back.

The road became increasingly rutted. She held on to the grip above her head and tightened her seat belt.

"Not long now," Tony said.

They arrived at the end of the dirt road. He parked under the shade of a tree and waited at the front of the SUV for her to join him. He held the No Admittance tape up while they ducked under it.

After walking up a shallow arroyo they came upon a cliff. It was not as high as the one back at the village but beautiful in its pastel desert colors. She could see the stone buildings partially revealed under the talus that had fallen on the dwellings over a long period of time.

A shiver danced down her spine as she realized they were the only two living people there. The wind whispered through a copse of willows and cottonwoods, sounding like the sibilant groans of ghosts who still occupied the site.

"You hear it, too," he said.

"What?"

"The voices of the dead."

The hair stood up on her arms. She rubbed the chill away and stepped out of the shadow of the trees into the sun. "It's an eerie place." She spoke in a soft voice.

He nodded. "Come on."

Taking her hand in his big warm one, he led the way over the rocky debris. She was glad she had on sturdy sneakers. The going was treacherous.

At the archeological dig, string marked depths and boundaries that had been explored. Tony muttered a curse.

"Anyone could walk in here and take anything they wanted," he said in disgust. "I told the site manager they needed evening and morning surveillance at the very least."

Around the side of the cliff, out of sight of the main research area, they found another pile of displaced stones. It was obviously the work of thieves, the digging showing signs of being hurried, the culprits uncaring of those items they destroyed in the process. Tony picked up several pieces and fitted them together into a partial vase. His face took on a grim expression.

Julianne laid a hand on his arm. "I'm sorry."

He shrugged before carefully wrapping the pieces in the shirt he removed, then he trudged on.

She couldn't help admiring the portrait he presented against the rugged landscape. He was built like one of the wild mustangs that roamed the West—lean but muscular, streamlined as one should be who raced the wind....

"The local tribes have been advising us on the excavating," he said after a couple of minutes of silence. "They believe each thing has its time. When that time is finished, whether for a village, tree, animal or person, it should be left to return to the earth. We're doing a very limited exploration here, then we'll backfill the ruins and leave them at rest."

They explored a couple of rooms that had been cleared before he unlocked a nearby trailer that held mostly potsherds and flint tools. There were photos of a few preserved baskets.

"Don't touch anything," he warned. "This site predates construction of the great houses," he explained. "It's an example of the early villages as clans moved into the canyon. It's called the Basketmakers III period. The name comes from the Pecos classification of Pueblo cultures."

"Isn't it unusual to find so many intact utensils?" she asked, looking the treasures over and resisting the urge to pick them up for a closer study.

"Yes. I think the people abandoned the site due to a significant rock fall. Lots of stuff got buried."

"Including people?"

"Surprisingly, we've found only a few bones." He opened a drawer to show her. "The families probably returned and dug up the dead for a proper burial."

"How humane."

"They were an advanced civilization. They knew how to farm. They stored food in baskets and pots that were art as well as craft. They built roads and traded goods far and wide."

Pulling on cotton gloves and giving her a pair, he pointed out designs and the signature marks that indicated the items were made by distinctive artisans.

"Look," he said, pointing to identical markings on two nearly complete pots and on a shard. "This means the wind. Whoever made these pieces called himself the wind."

"Or herself."

"Yes."

His dark eyes met hers. A smile flashed across his face. Her heart sprinted from normal to a mad rush in two seconds flat. Time stretched, a second into an hour, a minute into eternity. He moved, a slight bending of his head, then stopped.

She had to part her lips in order to breathe as yearning and expectation filled her chest like a spring storm. The wait became unbearable.

He blinked and moved away.

Disappointment replaced the confusing swirl of emotions. She turned blindly to the table of shards. "Maybe the artisan was your ancestor," she said in a husky voice. "Aquilon is the Spanish word for the north wind, isn't it?"

"The winter wind," he murmured in agreement.

A shiver prickled her scalp. She gazed at the pottery, feeling foolish for wanting…wanting something she couldn't put a name to.

"Did you notice this?" he asked, pointing to a basket with part of a woven lid still attached. "It's too fragile to handle now, but it was sturdy in its day. It held seed corn for the next year's planting."

"Fascinating," she murmured after they had gone around the entire room and admired everything. "I've run out of superlatives to describe the workmanship."

He stopped speaking and checked his watch. "I've been rattling on for nearly two hours," he said with a frown.

"I loved every minute. Thank you for allowing me to see this wonderful treasure."

An unreadable emotion flickered through his eyes, then he grinned ruefully. "I probably shouldn't have, especially since you're a prime suspect for dealing in stolen artifacts from this very spot."

Shock rippled through her. "Surely you realize I didn't know anything about those pots being stolen. Truly, I never even looked in the box to see what they were. Not that I would have known they were valuable antiques," she added honestly.

He hooked his thumbs in his belt and studied her, long enough to make her uncomfortable.

"What?" she finally said.

"Unless we find someone who can verify your story, we have only your word and a box of stolen goods that *you* delivered."

She stared at him in dismay and anger. Anger won out. "You won't find my fingerprints on those pots," she informed him coldly. "I'm your link to the

couple. Only they can tell you who they were
fencing the property for."

"Fencing," he repeated. "You know the term."

"Yeah, I used to read my brothers' mystery
novels." She stalked out of the trailer, then realized
she was at his mercy for a ride. She waited by the
SUV for him to take her home, grimly aware that she
was no closer to clearing her name than she'd been
at the beginning of the trip.

But she was perilously closer to the abyss that
lurked in the attraction she felt toward the man who
showed his doubt of her innocence in every glance.

Chapter Four

Never in five years of law enforcement had Tony reacted this way to a suspect.

Distance, he reminded himself grimly the next morning. He had to keep the proper professional distance, no matter how lovely her smiles were, no matter how tender her eyes when she spoke of babies and families.

For a second, reminded of home and family, he missed the closeness and laughter of his foster uncle's house, the sense of belonging to people who cared. Glancing around his barracks-type quarters, he grimaced at how impersonal it was.

There were no decorative touches such as at Julianne's place with her vases of dried grass, pottery filled with pretty stones and shells, colorful prints on the walls. The cottage was a home rather than just a place to sleep.

Thinking of her reminded him of the case. The tribal elder had thought the charges against her should be dropped. He and the women of the NAWAC obviously loved and respected Julianne. However, because he was working with the local police and the attempted sale of the artifacts had happened in their jurisdiction, the county D.A. had the final say on dismissing the case against her.

Tony wondered briefly if he should attempt to have the case moved, either to the tribe or to the federal court since the site was on park service land.

On what grounds? That she seemed honest and open? That she had friends who cared enough to come to her defense?

Or was it that he was attracted to her?

The erotic dreams about the lovely suspect hadn't cooled down one iota, so he had to consider his own motives for wanting to believe her besides her earnest manner as she tried to help him find the couple and her obvious dismay at their disappearance.

Swinging out of bed and heading for the shower, he heard the wind in the cottonwoods. It seemed to whisper a secret for his ears alone.

Julianne.

He liked her name. Also her obvious intelligence, her independence, the way she'd defended herself, fighting him off like a cornered cat. For a second he considered the interlude in the artifact trailer, the nearly overpowering desire to kiss her, to taste those delicately curved lips.

She'd felt it, too.

The intensity had alarmed him.

Her interest in the artifacts hadn't been feigned. Neither had he seen greed flicker in her eyes as it sometimes did with others who beheld the treasures. Again understanding had flowed between them as they'd examined the pieces from the past.

It was a good thing he hadn't given in to the impulse to kiss her, after all. Too many things stood between them. First was the case and her involvement.

Second, he wasn't sure he was cut out for any kind of lasting relationship. His own father had walked out when he was three. His stepfather, a fun, laughing man whom he'd loved, had moved the family around a lot, traveling the rodeo or roundup circuits.

Which was why his mom had finally bailed out. She'd wanted the security of a permanent home and a husband who was around to share it.

Restless spirits, she'd called his father and step- father. It was in their genes or souls or whatever governed their lives.

Since living with his stepuncle, he'd seen the

value of a regular home and realized its importance for a family.

Wives and kids needed stability. His job kept him moving to wherever he was needed. He would never give it up, so he, too, must have the restless spirit that had so bothered his mother. That's why marriage and a family were out for him.

At six-thirty he was on the road. Passing the adobe cottage out on the highway, he noted Julianne's compact car under the lean-to carport. When he saw a light on inside, he struggled with a strong urge to stop.

Shaking his head as if to negate the impulse, he drove on. At the main dig site, he found the expert from the tribal museum on hand, checking over the pieces reclaimed by the university students who worked diligently with dental picks and brushes.

An air of earnest labor and intense interest permeated the atmosphere. When he finished his dissertation on the Early Basketmaker culture, he would be awarded a Ph.D. He had two goals in his career: to protect the ancient sites and to advance knowledge of the early cultures of North America. Being in the park service gave him access to many old sites, and the doctorate would give him the necessary authority in the field to be taken seriously.

"Life is more than work and school," his uncle had scolded the last time he visited the family back in Idaho.

Uncle Jeff was a happily married man, his wife

of the past thirteen years a spirited, caring woman who'd made the wounded veteran's life complete. His uncle wanted the same for the orphans he'd taken in, none of whom had yet found their soul mates.

Julianne.

The name flashed into his mind, and with it, a longing that caused heat to flare in that cold place inside him. He thought of having a family, a comfortable cottage to come home to at the end of a long day, lighted windows flashing a welcome, a loving woman waiting. He wanted to be able to share passion and dreams, but only with that special person, the soul mate his uncle told him everyone had.

He cursed silently. What the hell was he thinking? A brief, satisfying fling was one thing, but he had no time—or desire—to pursue romance and commitment.

Tony took a deep breath of the fresh morning air as a chill penetrated his heart. He had no idea where his biological father was or if the man was even alive, and he didn't care either way. That part of his life was over.

A memory of his early childhood came to him— the moving from place to place, changing schools, leaving friends behind. He would never put a wife and kids through that misery. Later, after his mother was killed in an accident, he and Krista had been placed in foster care, another type of hell. He cursed and determinedly put the past out of his mind as he headed for the archeological excavation.

Dr. Bruce Jones, curator of the Chaco Culture Museum and the man in charge of the site, hailed him. "Hey, Tony. I heard you'd made an arrest on the stolen artifacts case. Was it anybody we know?"

"Yeah. In fact, she mentioned you as a reference."

The doctor's eyes widened at this news. "Who?"

"Julianne Martin."

A welter of emotion rushed through Tony at the male interest that leaped into Bruce's eyes. He realized the doctor wasn't more than forty, if that much. He was also divorced and therefore perfectly free to be interested in the available females in the area. Julianne was easily the best-looking one around.

"Julianne wouldn't steal," Bruce stated. Another thought came to him. "Good Lord, you didn't put her in jail, did you?"

Without waiting for an answer, he headed toward the parking area and his pickup.

"She's okay," Tony advised. "Her brother and one of the tribal elders got her out. The NAWAC also put in an appearance on her behalf."

Bruce smiled at this news. "I know Cal. He's a good attorney."

Tony concealed his surprise that the museum curator knew Julianne's family.

"I'm glad that's straightened out," Bruce continued. "No one in his right mind would think Julianne capable of crime. She's the most honest person I've ever known. How come you arrested her?"

Tony tried not to sound defensive. "She tried to pass some artifacts from the dig at the store. She said she'd brought them in for some couple. She delivered their baby last week."

The site supervisor/artifact curator frowned. "I hope you catch them. This raiding of the ancient settlements has got to stop."

Tony felt this last complaint was directed at him. "I need to look over the other site," he said, suppressing irritation that everyone was so damn sure of Julianne's innocence.

Ignoring his own gut feeling in the matter, he went to the new site and spoke with the park ranger who'd patrolled the area since dawn. "No problems," the young man reported.

Afterward he stopped by the park manager's office.

Dick Worth was sixty, a dedicated public servant who loved his job. He'd had a heart attack last year, but that hadn't slowed him down. Dick was the one who'd noticed artifacts were missing and requested help.

"I've put a man out there," he told Tony, "but I can't keep someone on-site all the time. Our funds were cut again and we can't raise entrance prices."

Too little time, too little money, too much work. Those were a constant in the park service. Tony had known the problems when he'd chosen to make this field his career.

"Maybe I can squeeze something out of the tribal council to keep things going here," he said. "They

may be able to guard the digs while we're researching and cataloging the finds."

The ranger's face cheered up. "That would be
great."

"I'll ask," Tony said. "I can't promise."

"I understand."

They discussed plans and an escort to take the artifacts to the museum laboratory for formal study
and classification. After checking with Bruce on a
time, Tony left to cruise the canyon for possible
clues to the culprits.

He glanced at the radio clock on the truck's panel.
At lunch, he would drop by the district attorney's
office and see what the situation was with Julianne.
Julianne.

With a frown, he realized he thought of her that way,
as if she were someone he'd known nearly forever.

He wondered if she'd gone out to deliver a baby
that morning. That funny clutching feeling attacked
his chest again. It immediately swept down to his
groin. Memories of their struggle dashed through his
mind. He recalled every sensation, every touch—

"Chill," he muttered savagely and put all thoughts
of her out of his mind.

Late Tuesday Julianne closed the drug safe, spun
the cylinder and made sure the office was ready for
the next day. She was the last person out, and it was
her duty to see that all was secure. After one more

check of the premises, she locked the dead bolt and went to her car.

Stretching, she breathed deeply of the cool desert air. They'd had a brief rain that afternoon. The dust had settled and the scent of sage and cactus filled the air with a fresh, wonderful aroma. Twilight filled the sky with soft color, as if the fragrance were made visible in the pastels of evening.

Back at the cottage, she experienced a restless need that defied the fatigue of a long day. It had taken almost twelve hours to get through the patients who'd waited to have their ills tended. She'd called the doctor twice to verify symptoms and treatment and had referred one case to him for possible surgery.

After changing to jeans, a T-shirt and sneakers, she left the yard and walked along the edge of the arroyo that ran in a jagged path behind the house. The rain had puddled in a few places, but it hadn't been enough to become a flow.

A warning flooded her mind as she thought of Tony and their interactions over the weekend. Looking back, it all seemed rather bizarre.

That moment hadn't been like her at all. She wasn't instantly attracted to anyone. Perhaps her caution was due to the trauma of finding her home invaded and her mother violated, but her trust had to be built slowly, day by day, until she felt she knew the other person well.

But she was drawn to him in some elemental way she couldn't describe, except that it went deep, to some part of her she'd thought couldn't be reached. The hunger was unexpected for both of them.

She liked life to proceed on an orderly track so she had time to think things through. This was not the case in the attraction between them. It bewildered and overpowered her senses, leaving her longing for his touch and his kiss. One thing she knew—an uncontrollable rush of passionate need couldn't be good.

Pushing the tormenting circle of thought aside, she spotted two coyotes drinking from a puddle before they ran off at an easy lope across the landscape. An owl landed in a mesquite, looked her over, then turned his head with obvious disinterest in the human.

A low *whuff* penetrated the silence, a cross between a woof and a grunt. From experience she recognized the beat of wings from a large bird. Following the direction of the sound, she observed as a huge crow settled on the sand, then waddled importantly to the small pool of water for a drink and a ducking. Another crow joined the first one.

Loneliness surrounded her the way the deep purple aura of approaching night enfolded the landscape. Crossing her arms over the odd ache in her chest, she decided she would call her father. Talking to him always made her feel better.

Also her brother. As an attorney, Cal could advise

her on what to expect if she actually had to go to court. The more she knew about and understood the proceedings the more composed she would be when she faced the judge.

Entering the house, she dialed Cal first thing. "Hey, Jules," he answered before she could say anything.

"I hate caller ID," she muttered.

"These are modern times," he told her, laughter in his deep voice. "How's it going out there?"

"Well, the officer who arrested me says it's up to the D.A. about dropping the charges."

"Didn't the judge give a release order to the jail?"

"Yeah, but I think I'm still a prime suspect."

"I'll talk to the D.A., so don't worry about it."

"That's easy for you to say. You're not the one under suspicion," she informed him.

"So, what else is happening?"

"The, uh, arresting officer is an interesting character. He's some sort of antiquities expert and special investigator for the park service. Tony Aquilon. Have you heard of him?"

"Not that I recall. What's interesting about him?"

She sighed. "I don't know."

"He must be heart-stoppingly handsome. Like me," he added wickedly.

"Well, he's tall and dark, but he usually wears a scowl. Except when he's looking at something from an ancient culture, then he's entranced."

"Do I detect a hint of jealousy?"

Heat ran up her neck at her older brother's question. She recalled the moment in the trailer, the intensity, the flicker of desire in those dark eyes. "Hardly."

"Take care, little sis," he advised.

"Yeah, right. I've learned there's more to a man than a pretty face. You would do well to remember that, too." They discussed family matters for a few minutes, then she told him goodbye. "Love you, even if you are my most annoying relative."

Laughing, he returned her farewell and hung up.

Sitting on the porch so she could enjoy the twilight, she called her father. "How's it going?" she asked.

"Fine," he replied as usual.

"Same here. Now that we've finished with the polite lies, how are you, really?"

"No problems. Really. I'm walking every day just as the doctor ordered. My medicine is working great, so no more pain. Now, what's your problem?"

"Problem?" she said, flustered.

"I can always tell by your voice. Your mother got that little tremor when she was troubled about something. Of course, she also got it when she was madder than a hen with a rustled nest."

She loved her father's folksy sayings although they were contradicted by the fact that he taught physical therapy and did research at the university level.

"Did Cal tell you I was arrested for trying to sell native artifacts from a Chaco dig?"

"Yes, he mentioned the incident when we talked last night, but he said it wasn't a big deal. Do we now have a jailbird in the family?"

Concern underlay the humor in his rumbling voice.

"Not yet. Cal thinks all is resolved. The man who arrested me thinks not. Have you ever heard of Tony Aquilon? He's a special investigator with the park service."

"Then he should know how things stand with the case."

"He says the D.A. will have to decide if the charges are strong enough to go to trial. Right now, I'm out on bail, thanks to Cal, the tribal council and NAWAC. Tony, the investigator, and I are trying to find the couple who gave me the pots."

"Good. I'm sure this will soon be over. Do you want me to go to the hearing with you?"

"No, no," she assured him, her manner far more confident than she felt. "I'll be fine."

They talked for a few more minutes before saying goodbye. After hanging up, she experienced the loneliness again. She missed her family and the friends she'd known all her life, she realized.

After considering the alternatives, she thought she should call Diana Sheppard, a legal aide for the tribe and one very sharp lady. Maybe Diana knew something about the young couple who'd suckered *her* into their crime. Perhaps she could help find them and clear Julianne's name, assuming the D.A. decided not to believe her story.

If not, would the handsome investigator testify against her? Yes, she answered the question. She had an intuitive knowledge he would tell the truth no matter what the consequences were to anyone, including himself.

And the truth was she had delivered stolen goods to his shop and had agreed to take a thousand dollars for them. And each of those acts was a felony.

"Ohh," she groaned, pressing a hand to her aching head at her gullibility.

"My, you certainly had a busy weekend," Diana commented at lunch the next day, after Julianne told her all that had happened.

The two women had met a couple of months after Julianne had moved to Gallup. Diana worked with juvenile cases involving Native Americans.

Julianne had been impressed with the other woman's ability when they had both spoken up for a teenager who'd stolen food for his sick mother. Diana had arranged for a job for the boy in the grocery after school so he could repay his debt and buy the food his family needed.

"It was different from any I'd ever experienced," Julianne agreed wryly. "Do you have any ideas on how to find the couple?"

Diana shook her head. "If they'd paid with a credit card at the clinic, we could trace its use. If they're living on the reservation, they're supposed to let the tribal office know."

"My hearing is Monday. I wish I could find them before then and get my name cleared. Even if the charges against me are dropped, I don't like the idea of a cloud of suspicion trailing after me. Some people would always wonder about my innocence."

"I wouldn't like that, either."

When the waitress came to their table, Julianne ordered the day's special, then waited as her companion asked some questions about the luncheon menu. She glanced around the busy restaurant, nodding to a couple she recognized.

"I met someone last week," Diana said, changing the subject. "A friend introduced us."

"An interesting man?" she asked, giving the other woman an opening to talk if she wanted. They'd spent enough time on her problems.

"Well, handsome, at any rate. We've only spoken a couple of times. I'm wondering if he may be able to help you. He's really smart."

Julianne thought of the financial consultant she'd dated shortly after her arrival in the area. He'd been smart, but there'd been something callous about him.

Or maybe that was just her imagination.

At any rate, he'd pushed her too hard about

having a relationship before she was ready. She hadn't liked that. So she'd refused his invitations.

"Why do you think this man can help?" she asked Diana.

"He's with the National Park Service and works with the archeologist up at the Chaco Canyon site. He could probably get a list of the workers who've helped with the dig. Maybe one of them was the thief."

Julianne suspected she already knew the person and that he wasn't likely to give her the time of day, much less any valuable information.

Diana continued, "Josiah could have worked there and stolen the pots on his own. Or maybe he had a relative at the site who acted as his supplier."

Julianne nodded and tried not to look glum.

"Anyway, the man I met is staying in the barracks over at park headquarters until he has a chance to find an apartment. He'll be stationed here for the foreseeable future, he said. You should call there and see if he has any ideas on Josiah."

"What's his name?"

"Tony Aquilon. I may have the headquarters phone number written on something." She searched in her purse.

Julianne groaned inwardly. "Never mind," she told her friend. "I know how to reach him."

Chapter Five

On Friday morning Julianne made the long drive to tribal headquarters. Her report was neatly typed and ready for review by the council. During the past month, she'd seen a record number of cases during open-clinic days and had delivered eighteen babies: seven at home, the other eleven either in the clinic outpatient center or at the local hospital for those patients who had complications.

Eighteen deliveries. A very busy month.

She smiled as she pulled into a parking space and cut the engine. Once inside the sprawling adobe building, she got a cup of coffee and headed for the conference room.

At the door she heard a familiar voice. Her hand jerked in surprise. Wary, she pushed the heavy door open and entered the room.

All eyes turned to her, but only one pair made her heart speed up and every nerve in her body tingle.

Tony Aquilon.

For a second, she wished they'd met under other circumstances. Then they could get to know each other without suspicion and doubts between them.

Chief Windover gestured for her to come in. She did so reluctantly. Forcing a smile, she nodded to the council members, then took in the others gathered around the long table. Tony Aquilon was one. So was Diana Sheppard. The third was Edmund Franks, financial advisor to the council and the man she'd dated briefly during the spring.

"Please be seated," the chief said. "The financial meeting of the council will now come to order. The first item of business is the budget report."

The tribal treasurer referred to a stack of notes and advised them that nearly every department was over their allowable expenses, including the clinic.

"Julianne, do you have a report ready?" Chief Windover asked. He reminded her of her father, a kind, easygoing man who wasn't afraid of responsibility. "I understand last weekend was pretty interesting."

"*Harrowing* is the word that comes to my mind," she told him while passing around copies of her report.

Most of those present laughed—but not Tony.

"Thanks for coming to my rescue," she continued, resuming her seat and picking up her copy of the report. "I thought I would have to spend the weekend in jail. Not that it wasn't a fascinating experience," she added ruefully, "but I had other things to do."

"Tony says you have a hearing on Monday," the chief said. "Naturally I'll be available to vouch for you if need be. We can't have our best midwife locked up, not with all these babies to attend to." He glanced at the report. "Eighteen in one month. It must have been a snowy winter."

That elicited another round of laughter. Julianne couldn't help but grin, too. She would love to have children of her own with someone special....

Her breath caught as her gaze went to Tony, seated across the table from her. His thoughts were inscrutable, but there was something compelling in his eyes. Desire? Distrust? Both? She couldn't tell and forced herself to look away.

It was odd to be so attracted to a man who had every reason to doubt her innocence. After all, she had delivered the stolen goods. She sighed and turned her attention to the meeting.

Edmund spoke up. "The clinic is over its budget on all supplies and medicines."

"We've had a large caseload recently. Some patients are having difficulty meeting the copayments. One of the mining companies shut down, and tourism has slowed due to gasoline prices."

She diligently answered each question about the medical facility and discussed ways to make it more efficient.

"Can you cut staff?" Edmund asked.

She gave him a level stare. "No. I have only one registered and two practical nurses on duty. They already work ten hours a day with no extra pay. Some days we have to stay twelve hours to get through the patient load."

Chief Windover sighed. "We can't cut down on clinic hours. We're already down to three days."

After an hour, the council decided to continue with the current plan while searching for other sources of revenue.

Diana gave her report next. Her office was also overworked and understaffed. "Education is vital. We have to come up with a program to keep the kids in school and to fund scholarships for college. Otherwise, we're going to have more juvenile delinquency and crime."

Edmund suggested the schools hold more fundraising activities. "Perhaps the tribe should get a percentage of the receipts from Chaco Canyon." He glanced at Tony with a challenge in his eyes.

"The park service is as strapped for cash as the council," Tony told them. "I was going to request help from the tribal police to guard the new archeological dig. Items are being stolen because we don't have enough surveillance."

The council voted to keep one officer at the site during the week, until the research was completed and the ruins buried again. Weekends were too busy and all officers were needed for other duties.

The meeting ended shortly before noon. Julianne, Tony and Diana walked out together. She was quiet as the three of them strolled toward the parking lot, Diana and Tony chatting in an easy manner.

"Hey, how about lunch?" a masculine voice called.

She turned as Edmund caught up with her. She would really prefer to go home and stay there. Alone.

Although he was a handsome man with a take-charge manner that some women probably found appealing, he didn't bowl her over. In fact, she'd felt somewhat uneasy around him since she'd declined to go out with him after a few dinner dates six months ago. With her caseload, as she'd explained, she didn't have time for a relationship.

"Good idea," Tony seconded the suggestion before she could refuse. "Where would you ladies like to go?"

Diana named a popular restaurant that was only a block away, and they decided to walk. The foursome went in pairs with Tony and Diana leading the way.

"It's nice to see you again," Edmund said as they strolled along the pleasant street shaded by eucalyptus trees. "I'd begun to think you were avoiding me."

"Not at all. I was involved with deliveries during the last meeting. I assume you got my report."

"Yes." He held the door for her as they entered the dim, cool restaurant. "I'm going to be at the clinic for a few days next week in order to study your operations."

"Why?" she asked, surprised and displeased at this news. She didn't like being spied on.

Moreover, she wished she'd never agreed to go out with him during the two months they'd dated, but she was only human. He was good-looking, with gray eyes, light brown hair and a quick grin. He'd been attentive, and she'd been somewhat lonely, being away from her family and old friends for the first time since finishing college.

That had been a mistake on her part, going with someone she hadn't known a very long time. When he'd pressed for a more-intimate involvement, she'd withdrawn. At the time, he'd been angry. Now he was all smiles and charm again. She wondered why.

Glancing at Tony, she decided she liked a man to be straightforward in their dealings. *He* certainly didn't practice any wiles on her.

She experienced a twinge inside as she observed the ease with which he and Diana were talking. There seemed to be no hidden tensions between them. If she and Tony had met in an ordinary way, would they have enjoyed that effortless companionship?

A part of her told her they wouldn't. There was something more between them—

"The council wants to see if we can't streamline some of the services they provide," Edmund clarified.

"Or cut them out altogether?" she questioned. "That would mean going to the emergency room for deliveries and no prenatal care."

As financial advisor, he had a great deal of influence with the council. She knew that, and it worried her. He could convince them to close the clinic entirely when her contract was up.

"I can see you don't think that's a good idea," he said as they were ushered to a table by the hostess.

"Shutting down the clinic would be a terrible mistake," she said flatly.

"Are they thinking of doing that?" Tony asked.

"We're looking for ways to cut expenses," Edmund explained to the other two. He smiled at Diana. "I'll be auditing your department after I finish at the clinic."

Her manner was completely confident. "I hope you'll remember that teenage crime is down by a third since we started the advocacy program to intercept problems before they became something bigger."

"I'll remember," he promised. He turned to Julianne. "Do you need a character witness when you have your day in court? After I check the clinic's books, I'm sure I'll be able to vouch for your integrity in the handling of the finances there."

Julianne had never had her word questioned before that ridiculous arrest, but now she seemed to be under siege from all sides. Or was it just her morbid imagination?

"I don't know." Her troubled gaze went to Tony. He observed her without expression, which caused her heart to give a little lurch of alarm. "What about you?" she asked, forcing a light note. "Will you vouch for my good character?"

He shrugged. "I'll tell the judge you cooperated in trying to find the couple you say gave you the stolen pots to deliver."

Her heart gave another lurch, bigger this time. It sounded as if the special investigator didn't believe her story. Despite her brother's confidence the other day, she wasn't sure it was going to be so easy to get the case against her dismissed. It was very dispiriting to be considered a crook.

"Anybody can see Julianne's innocent," Diana stated, evidently seeing no problem. "On a happier note, let's plan a cookout at my place for Sunday. It's so warm, I thought we could swim, then grill some hamburgers. Would five o'clock be a good time for everyone?"

"That works for me," Edmund said. "Would you like me to pick you up?" he asked Julianne.

"I can drive myself," she said, realizing she'd made a commitment to attend. Well, she wouldn't have hurt Diana's feelings by refusing, but she really didn't think this was a good idea. She didn't want to become part of a foursome that included her and Edmund as a possible couple.

"Tony?" Diana questioned.

"Uh, yeah, I can make that," he said. His smile flashed bright and friendly at the other woman.

Julianne was troubled by an unfamiliar emotion. During the remainder of the luncheon, while the conversation veered to television shows and a movie being made over in Monument Valley, she tried to figure out what was bothering her.

Her attention only partly engaged as Diana gestured animatedly while telling an amusing story about nearly being an extra on a movie set, Julianne concluded her best interests lay in clearing her name and that was the main thing to concentrate on. She had to be above suspicion to justify the trust Chief Windover and the council, also the NAWAC, had in her.

Proving her innocence would also show Special Investigator Aquilon that he'd been wrong to arrest her for a crime she hadn't been aware of committing. If he'd asked how she acquired the pottery instead of taking her to jail, things would have been different between them.

"You're quiet," Edmund remarked.

Julianne managed a wry smile. "I was thinking of crime and punishment, as in, can a person be blamed for a crime she didn't know she was committing?"

Edmund leaned close. "I'll help you prove your innocence," he promised.

"If she's innocent, she won't need any help," Tony said. "All we need to do is find the missing couple."

"I am innocent," she informed him, suppressing an urge to pound that message into his suspicious mind.

He nodded as if he believed her, which made her feel good for about ten seconds, until he told her, "You'll have to convince the district attorney."

Giving him a deadpan stare and speaking sardonically, she said, "That makes me feel so much better."

"The D.A. is out to make a name for himself," Edmund told her, a worried frown on his handsome face. "He plans to run for a seat in congress. He may make this a showcase trial."

"How?" Diana asked.

Tony explained. "A lot of people feel strongly about preserving native artifacts and ancient cultures, but there are collectors who don't care where the art comes from. They just want a piece of it."

"So they can claim they have something no one else has," Julianne added. "It's a selfish attitude."

"But human," Edmund said, leaning back in his chair while the waitress refilled their iced-tea glasses. His manner was sympathetic.

Julianne wondered if perhaps she had misjudged him in the past. Maybe he'd felt more for her than she'd realized when she'd thought he was pushing for more than she wanted to give. Glancing up, she met the dark, thoughtful gaze of the man who'd arrested her.

"I'll find Josiah and get to the truth," she declared, "if it's the last thing I do."

"Stay out of it," Tony advised coolly. "You get in my way, and I'll lock you up."

The other two looked rather shocked at his statement.

Julianne gave him a challenging smile. "You'll have to catch me first."

Julianne was up and dressed early on Saturday morning. She had two days to find Josiah and get this whole mess cleared up before her hearing at ten on Monday, so she wanted to get an early start.

After sweeping the polished concrete floor and dusting the furniture, she was ready to head out to the Chaco Canyon site. Dr. Bruce Jones was in charge of the dig, and she'd arranged to meet him there.

Bruce, looking very much like his student volunteers, spotted her immediately upon her arrival.

"Julianne, good morning," he called, rushing forward to open the car door. "You're just in time. We've found a new level at the site. I thought you might be interested."

They jumped in his pickup and bounced down the rough road to the new place that Tony had taken her to, the one where the artifacts had been stolen.

"To see something for the first time in nearly a

thousand years is exciting," she said, keeping pace with his long stride as they walked the last quarter mile over rocky terrain to the ancient ruins.

Her heart speeded up when she recognized a park service vehicle under the shade of a cottonwood farther up the narrow side canyon. Bruce took her hand when they got to the big boulders at the bottom of the talus area. They clambered up and around the bend until they reached the ruins.

Several students crowded around Bruce, all talking at once. Julianne followed them to the rectangular hole they'd excavated. Tony, she noted, was in it, his attention focused on a clay pot he was very slowly, very carefully freeing from the rocky soil. At last he held it up so everyone could see that it was in one piece. A cheer went up.

Dark eyes spotted her when she moved to one side for a better view. His eyebrows went up as if he questioned her presence there. She stuck her chin out and gave him a defiant smile.

"I think you two have met," Bruce said with a hint of amusement in his words.

"What's she doing here?" Tony wanted to know.

"I had an appointment with Bruce, with Dr. Jones," she informed him, switching to Bruce's title as if that gave her authority to be there. She didn't have to ask her captor for permission, did she?

"Easy, easy," Bruce said, taking the exquisite piece of pottery when Tony held it up to him. "This is great, only one chip out of the bottom edge. See if you can spot it," he told Tony.

"It isn't here that I can see." Tony hoisted himself out of the chamber, which was six feet below the surface where they'd already explored. "Let's take it to the trailer and clean it up."

Bruce directed the team in excavating at the new level. Julianne was impressed with their care. The workers diligently put in pegs and tied strings to them to measure each level of rock and dirt they removed. The debris had to be carried in buckets to a safe place at the bottom of the slope for dumping.

"Come on," Bruce said to her, holding out his hand to help her down the boulders.

She was aware of Tony at her back on the way to the trailer. Bruce unlocked the door and the three went inside. The shelves were empty.

She gasped. "Did someone break in? Were all the artifacts stolen?"

"No, no," Bruce assured her. "We moved everything to the museum basement this week. Uh, have you been in the trailer? We don't usually allow anyone inside."

Julianne's eyes locked with Tony's. She was sure they looked as guilty as kids caught sneaking forbidden snacks.

"I brought her out last weekend," he admitted. "We were looking for the couple who gave her the stolen goods."

"Ah," the curator said in understanding. "Julianne wants a list of everyone who works at the site. Let's catalog the pot, then go to the office."

Julianne didn't miss the black scowl Tony shot her way. He definitely wasn't pleased. Tough. This was her reputation on the line. She'd decided to follow Diana's advice and see if she could trace anyone at the site to the couple.

Standing quietly to one side, she waited until the men finished photographing the artifact and had tagged it. Tony stored it on a shelf after wrapping it in protective netting that was attached to the wall.

To her discomfort, he followed Bruce's pickup back to the park headquarters building. And stuck to them like glue as they went to Bruce's office.

Bruce picked up several pieces of paper from his desk. "Here's the list you wanted." He held the report out to her.

Tony easily overreached her and took the typed sheets. "These are the names of everyone who's worked at the site of the new find?"

"Yes." Bruce glanced from one to the other. "I suppose you're working together on this."

"No," Tony said.

"Yes," Julianne said at the same time. She gave her nemesis a severe frown and held out her hand for the list. "Diana gave me the idea of checking the volunteers for any connection to Josiah—"

"That could be dangerous," Tony interrupted, waving the list under her nose. "This is my case. *I'll* do the investigating."

"Have you come up with any leads?" she demanded.

"I, uh, can get an extra copy," Bruce stated with more than a hint of laughter in his eyes. "If you'll give me that one."

Tony handed the list of names over. Bruce excused himself and left the office. From down the hall, they heard the sound of a copy machine.

"You'll stay out of this," Tony ordered.

"So what have you been doing all week?" she asked. "You haven't found Josiah. At least, I'm running down some possible leads."

"For your information, I'd already asked for a complete list, including those who are no longer working on-site."

"Oh."

"Yeah, oh," he mimicked. He touched his nose as if recalling their first meeting.

"Your nose looks fine," she told him. "And most of the discoloration under your eyes is gone, too."

"No thanks to you," he muttered.

"I didn't ask to be accosted," she reminded him.

He got in her face. "If I ever accost you, you'll know it. I was as careful with you as I could be…given the circumstances."

"Oh, yes, I was a dangerous crook that you had

to handcuff in order to haul off to jail," she mocked, all her grievances with him pouring over her like a spring flood.

His shrug was insouciant. "What was I supposed to do—ask nicely that you put the handcuffs on and come along like a good girl? Besides, you were the one who lunged at me and wouldn't be still."

"That was self-defense and you know it."

"Uh," Bruce said from the open doorway, "I have the extra copy of the names."

Julianne spun away from Tony. She felt heated and overwrought and ridiculous. She accepted the copy. "Thank you for your help," she said with a great deal of graciousness in her manner. "I'll be on my way."

With one last fulminating glance over her shoulder, she sailed out of the office, got in her car and left with a defiant spray of gravel. After nearly going through the roof when she hit a pothole, she slowed down and fastened the seat belt. She had to figure out what to do next.

Tony gave Julianne a head start since he didn't want to eat her dust the whole way from the canyon to the paved road. At her speed, she was throwing up a cloud that could be seen from Ship Rock.

He gave a snort. She was the most mule-headed woman he'd ever met. And she was angry.

So was he.

He had a thing or two to say to her about interfering in an investigation. And he needed to talk to her about a meeting he'd arranged with the district attorney on Monday morning. If all went well, there wouldn't be a court case.

Once on the highway, he sped up until he had Julianne in sight. To his annoyance she didn't go home. Instead she turned north at the main road.

Thirty minutes later she stopped at a gas station. "Are you following me?" she demanded when he pulled in beside her and got of the SUV.

"I have a good reason." He frowned when he heard how defensive he sounded.

They glared at each other.

"I need to talk to you," he at last said when it was obvious she wasn't going to back down. "Let's go inside."

To his surprise she didn't argue. Inside the building were a market and deli. Three tables, none of which were in use, lined one wall.

Tony ordered coffee for himself and a soda for Julianne after asking her preference.

"What do you want?" she asked when they were seated opposite each other.

Several ideas flashed into his head, but he didn't think she would be receptive to any of them. He had to smile. This case was different from any other he'd ever worked on. He'd never been consumed by a desire to make mad love to a suspect before.

"What's funny?" she demanded, eyeing him suspiciously.

"Us," he said with a huskiness that made him silently groan. "Never mind," he added before she exploded. "I spoke with the D.A. this morning."

She at once became wary. "And?"

"We have a meeting in his office at nine on Monday."

"We, as in you and I?"

He nodded. "Since you're cooperating in the search for the thieves, he might offer you clemency—"

"To heck with clemency," she interrupted. "I'm not guilty of anything, unless you count trusting people a crime. I'd worked with that couple for eight months. They were so nice…"

The heat went out of her, and her voice trailed off into a sigh. Tony fought the instinct that made him want to pull her into his arms and tell her everything would be all right. That would be a really brilliant thing to do.

"Most people are nice when they want something," he told her. "You're old enough to know that."

Her gray eyes turned molten silver as anger flashed into them. "I know it very well. So what is it that *you* want?"

He realized he should have expected the question. "For you to cooperate by doing exactly what I tell you."

"Do I look like a puppet? I won't be manipulated

by you or anyone. I'll take my chances with a jury, if it comes to that."

When she stuck her chin out in challenge, all he could think of was the way her lips would feel under his. There were other uses besides the heat of anger for the passionate intensity she displayed.

"Stop it," she muttered.

He blinked and carefully smoothed all expression from his face. He revealed too much of what he was thinking when he was around her. That wasn't good. He finished the coffee and stood. "Nine o'clock Monday morning at the D.A.'s office. Got that?"

She nodded.

"Where are you going from here?" he asked, suspicious of her acquiescent manner.

"I have a birthing class at Ship Rock."

She met his gaze and held it, managing to look as pure as a cactus flower. Watch out for the barbs, he warned himself as he watched her leave.

Julianne noted the expressions of the fathers-to-be as they watched the film of an actual birth. It was her experience that the younger men observed the event as if memorizing the procedure for a test. The one older man in the group appeared embarrassed and kept his eyes on the floor more than on the screen.

How, she wondered, had something so natural gotten so isolated from the culture?

After the film, she had the couples practice their breathing exercises while she described what would be happening during the birth.

"Okay, we're in the rest cycle. What happens here?"

"Deep breaths," the older man answered, surprising her.

"That's right. This is the time to oxygenate the blood for the big push ahead. Okay, now we have a contraction starting. What do we do?"

"Check the time," one of the other men called out.

"Right. When should you come to the clinic?"

"When contractions are about five minutes apart."

"Or if the water breaks," one of the women spoke up.

"Right. Very good. Any questions about the process so far?" After going over a couple of points, Julianne dismissed the class of eight couples. "Mariah, Carlos, could I see you two for a moment?"

Mariah and her husband, a couple in their late thirties who were expecting their first child, stayed behind.

Julianne glanced at her records. "Your blood pressure is a little high. Did I give you the info on controlling it, the brochure about cutting back on salt, getting in a brisk walk and doing the relaxation techniques each day?"

"Yes, I am doing those things."

"Some of the time," Carlos added.

"I'm trying," Mariah said. "It's hard to add in more activities when I'm already working and taking care of our mothers."

"Having elderly parents and children to care for at the same time is a double whammy for many couples. Try to take some time for yourself," she advised her patient. "You need to stay healthy in order to help others. I'm writing a prescription for you—one twenty-minute rest with your feet up after lunch each day and a half-hour walk each evening."

"I don't have time," Mariah protested.

"You're to go with her on the walk," Julianne told the husband. "Set a comfortable pace. Make sure she gets eight hours of rest each night."

After the husband nodded, Julianne retrieved a picture from her purse and showed it to them. "Here's a photo I took of Josiah and Mary Pareo and their new baby. I think he is a cousin of yours?" she said to Mariah, knowing that Josiah's wife had referred the older couple to the clinic.

"He is my cousin," Mariah admitted.

"I helped with the birth of their new son, but now they seem to have disappeared. Do you have any idea where they might have gone?"

The husband and wife glanced at each other, then shrugged to indicate they didn't.

Julianne didn't know if they'd heard of her arrest. She decided to take a chance that they hadn't.

"Josiah asked me to deliver some pottery to the tourist shop in Gallup. I'm not sure what to do about the payment. When I went out to his place, his trailer was gone. If you see him, would you tell him to contact me? He knows when I'm at the clinic."

"Yes, I will do that. I will tell my aunt, too."

"Oh, does she live around here?"

Julianne found that Josiah's mother had a house a few miles south of Gallup. She decided to head home, eat lunch and check out the address that afternoon.

A sense of elation filled her as she drove down the highway at a fast clip. At last she was making real progress in solving her case.

Chapter Six

Tony entered the shop he'd leased over a month ago in an effort to break up the ring of thieves dealing in antiquities. So far he'd had no luck in locating the man Julianne claimed had given her the pottery.

Upon checking with the garage owner, he'd discovered Josiah had worked there during the summer but was let go in September when the tourist season dried up.

The twenty-one-year-old father also had a police record for stealing when he'd been a juvenile, a minor charge that had eventually been dropped. From this, Tony had gotten a mug shot, so he knew what the young man had looked like at sixteen.

"How's it going?" he said to the new clerk, who was arranging baskets on the totem-pole hat rack for display.

Sandra was Native American, eighteen and a very good worker. She'd already straightened up most of the shelves and dusted everything in the store. Her salary was a stretch for the amount of business they had. He supplemented it from the department's discretionary fund when necessary.

Her smile was huge. "I sold three blankets this morning. A teacher from California wanted them for her classroom. They're studying the old mission trail."

"Hey, that is great news. The merchandise looks a lot better," he complimented, glancing around the cluttered store. "You've done a good job at sorting things out."

"It was fun discovering new items hidden under the other stuff."

In the office he checked the cash register receipts, brought the ledgers up to date, then took the picture of Josiah out of his pocket and studied the young man's face as if searching for clues on locating him.

With a sigh, he admitted he would have to go to every garage within a hundred-mile radius—

"I know who that is," Sandra said. She handed him the extra cash from the earlier sale and pointed to the picture of Josiah. "Josiah's mother is my mom's best friend. They're cousins."

Tony smiled. Everyone who lived within two hundred miles of Gallup was a cousin to everybody else. It was a given for those who belonged to the local tribe. "Yeah? You know where his mother lives?"

She hesitated.

Tony knew no one liked to rat on a friend. "The store owes him money for some items."

Her shoulders relaxed. "She lives south of town. I'll draw you a map."

He handed her a notepad and a pen. She sketched the roads and the homestead he was to look for on the paper, giving him detailed instructions as she did.

"Go south on the highway and take the turnoff toward El Morro, but don't go there. You'll turn, um, left just past Ramah—you'll be heading toward Lookout Mountain, but don't go there, either. There's a dirt road past the lake—not the lake on this side of Ramah, but the one on the other side?"

He nodded patiently when she looked at him to see if he understood the directions. In this country of few roads and fewer signs, he knew to look for landmarks and to count dirt lanes to find the correct turn.

"There used to be a gas station and market on the corner here," she said, drawing a square on the sketch. "It burned down a couple of years ago."

He nodded again and wondered how women ever got to their destinations, given their inclination to toss in extra information that was no help at all.

"Turn right and keep going a few miles—I'm not very good at distances. It might be ten miles. Look for the mailbox. It has the name on the side of it." She smiled as if she'd just scored a hundred on an important test and handed him the notepad.

"Thanks. I'll head out there as soon as I get the bookkeeping out of the way." He tore off the top sheet and stuck it in his shirt pocket.

After finishing at the store, he picked up a bag of tacos, a large soda and a six-pack of water from the cantina, stopped to fill up the gas tank and headed south on Highway 32. Once out of town, the traffic was very light. He set the cruise control on seventy-five, guided the SUV with one hand and munched on a taco.

Shortly before the entrance to the El Morro National Monument, he took the road toward the mountain, then came to a corner where the remains of a burned building were evident.

With a wry chuckle to himself, he headed mostly northeast on a gravel road and checked the directions again after he was past the lake. Within thirty minutes he found the correct mailbox.

The driveway, a dirt track, led west from the county road. In the distance he could see the gleam of the sun off a metal roof. He retrieved the binoculars he kept in the glove box and checked the place out.

The home was a cinder-block house with a tidy

sand-and-gravel yard and several mesquite trees for shade. A coyote fence completely surrounded it. Hmm, that could mean the woman had a dog.

"Damn," he muttered.

He didn't want a dog barking and giving away his presence. His idea of keeping the house under surveillance for a few days might not produce the "person of interest" as officials called suspects nowadays, but it was worth a try.

After driving up the road another half mile, he stopped and consulted a topographical map of the area. Ah, there was an old road that circled back behind the Pareo home.

He took the left turn and drove slowly in order to keep the dust down. He knew from experience that a person could track a vehicle for miles as it traveled along a dusty road through the desert.

The ravine he'd spotted on the map was right where he'd expected it to be. He drove very carefully along its rocky bottom until he was near the house, then he parked.

Standing on the running board and using the binoculars, he found he was in a perfect position to observe the home without being spotted and had a clear view of both the front and back yards. The only thing he couldn't see was the carport on the other side of the house.

The homestead was quiet. No dogs in the yard that he could see. A border of flowers bloomed across the front, while an old-fashioned swing moved gently to and fro in the shade cast by a mesquite tree.

After observing the place for nearly an hour, he settled into the driver's seat, finished off the last taco and the soft drink, then swallowed half a bottle of water. That would have to serve as his dinner as well as lunch.

He would hide out until after nightfall in case someone showed up under cover of darkness.

Julianne studied the directions, put her car into gear and eased back onto the gravel road. She was later than she'd meant to be due to a medical emergency at the clinic. Then one of the expectant mothers had stopped by before she could close up and leave. An examination had revealed she was having some contractions, but wasn't yet ready for birthing. Finally Julianne had gotten some lunch, studied the maps of the countryside and set out on her own quest.

Now she was looking for the dirt road leading to Josiah's mother's place. It should be coming up soon.

Not that she expected him and Mary to be there. It would be stupid to hide out at such an obvious place. However, if she could convince the mother about the seriousness of the situation and also convey the fact that Julianne would go to bat for the young couple if they cooperated with the law, then maybe the couple would contact her.

A big *if,* she admitted.

She found the mailbox. The name was correct, so she turned down the gritty road toward the house she could see about a half mile along the road.

As she came closer, she saw the place was very tidy. There was even a border of flowers along the front of the house and a free-standing bench swing in the yard.

Boulders and rocks had been arranged in a dry creek pattern that wound through the enclosure. The coyote fence kept out four-footed intruders. She didn't see or hear a dog when she stopped outside the fence and turned off the engine. Silence immediately surrounded her.

The hair on the back of her neck stood up.

"Hello," she called.

Not a sound.

She called again. Since no dog appeared, she opened the gate and followed a stone path to the front door. A face peered at her from the small glass pane in the portal.

Startled, she stepped back, her foot missing the concrete stoop and turning painfully to the side as it hit the ground. She caught the support post of the overhanging roof and steadied herself.

"Hello," she said to the woman behind the door. "Are you Josiah's mother? I'm Julianne Martin, the midwife. I helped deliver their son recently."

The door opened, exposing a very slender woman

with long gray hair neatly braided and hanging down her back. Her face was as smooth as new parchment, her smile reserved. She glanced over her shoulder as if someone else was in the house, but Julianne didn't spot anyone.

"Yes?" the woman said. "How can I help you?"

"Mrs. Pareo?"

"Yes."

Julianne explained about delivering the pottery to the tourist store in town. "I'm sure Josiah didn't know the items were antiques. The expert investigating the case needs to know how Josiah·got the pots so they can trace them to the real culprits."

"My son makes his own pottery."

"Usually he does," Julianne agreed. "In this case, I think he was doing a favor for a friend. I really need to find him…if you can tell me where he's moved?"

"He's gone to his grandfather to help bring the sheep down before winter sets in."

"Where is his grandfather's place?"

"Not here."

"In the mountains near here?" Julianne asked.

Mrs. Pareo hesitated. "Black Mesa."

Julianne's heart sank. "That's in Arizona, isn't it?"

After a brief nod the woman slowly closed the door. "If I see Josiah, I will tell him to call you. I'm sorry. I cannot help you more."

Walking back to the car, all Julianne's bright

hopes of solving the case dried up as quickly as the puddles in the ravine did after a rain.

She retraced the track to the main road and headed home, her mind devoid of any ideas at all. All she could think of was the jail cell where she'd spent the night last Saturday. One week ago. It was frightening how much a life could change in such a short time.

It wasn't until she was back within the city limits of town that she realized she was being followed.

Her heart started to thump hard, then rapidly upped its rate when she stopped at a red light and identified the driver of the SUV tailing her.

What was wrong now?

Since she wasn't sure if she should pull over or what, and he gave no indication to help her out, she continued homeward. Tony followed her into the driveway and stopped an inch from her bumper.

Sucking in a harsh breath, she got out and faced the special investigator who was evidently hot on her trail.

Again.

"What?" she demanded as soon as he exited his vehicle, deciding to meet trouble head-on.

"That's my question," he informed her grimly. He stopped two feet from her and crossed his arms over his chest in the manner of a parent bent on inquisition.

She stared at him without responding.

"What the hell were you doing out at the Pareo place?"

The question took her aback. "Looking for

Josiah," she replied in the most reasonable tone possible. "What else would I be doing?"

He gazed at the late-afternoon sky as if seeking divine guidance. Her temper flared even as she determined to remain calm and stoic no matter what he said.

As if anything was ever calm between them, some part of her whispered with impish glee.

Directing a stern glare at her, he leaned forward slightly and demanded, "Do you realize you ruined any chance at all that I might catch him there?"

"No. How could I?" she continued when he rammed his thumbs in his belt and rocked back on his heels in obvious disgust with her. "You didn't tell me what you planned."

"I'm not supposed to," he said. "I'm the investigator in the case. I had the mother's house under surveillance."

"Oh." She put two and two together. "So that's how come you were following me."

"Yeah. I thought about shooting your tires out, but I'm probably not as good a shot as John Wayne."

She wrinkled her nose at him. "Nah, that would have been a Dirty Harry trick, I think."

"This is not a joke." Tony's jaw felt so stiff he could hardly speak. Looking at her full lips as she licked them in a nervous gesture, he had another idea.

He thrust a hand through his hair and sighed loudly. "You do drive a man to extremes," he muttered.

She touched his arm and then withdrew her hand. "I'm sorry," she said in a sincere manner.

"How did you know where the mother lived?" he asked, cooling down somewhat.

She explained she'd found out about the Pareo home south of town through one of the couples in her birthing classes. "I thought if I explained everything to Josiah's mother, she would tell me where they were and we—" she gestured to him and then herself "—could talk to them and find out who gave him the artifacts."

After she fell silent, he just stood there and looked at her. She licked her lips again.

He nearly groaned with the effort to ignore those sexy lips. "So?" he said after a long silence. "Did you find out where the couple went?"

She nodded.

He was dumbfounded. "You did? Where?"

"To his grandfather's sheep ranch. In Arizona."

Tony's enthusiasm dwindled. "Did she narrow it down a little bit?"

"Black Mesa."

"That's several hundred square miles of mountains."

"She said she couldn't help me more than that and closed the door."

At her woebegone and also apologetic expression, Tony had to quell a knee-jerk reaction to take her in his arms and console her. While it was now fairly obvious that she'd been merely doing a good deed for the young couple and wasn't a suspect, he still had a job to do, he reminded the part of him that turned to mush around her.

"Let's go inside," she suggested.

He followed her into the pleasant little house and was instantly reminded of the contentment of family life, if one was lucky enough to find it. She slipped her shoes off inside the front door.

Without thinking, he took off his hiking shoes, which he wore when he thought he might be sneaking through the brush, and set them beside her much smaller sneakers.

She gave him a thoughtful glance, then an approving smile. He frowned to let her know he wasn't through with the interrogation. However she was already going into the kitchen and didn't notice.

"I'll make some sangria," she told him. In a few minutes she handed him a tall glass of blended fruit juice and red wine. "My father says this is very good for the blood pressure. You look as if you could use it."

He noticed the sparkle in her eyes at that moment. "This isn't funny."

She sighed. "I know, but…well, it is in a way."

"What way?" he asked grumpily.

She ushered him outside to the patio. The coolness of evening had expelled the heat of the day from the shaded table and chairs. They both sat so they could see the arroyo as the softer hues of sunset stole over the landscape. "I love the twilight," she murmured.

"Yeah," he said. "So you were going to tell me what you find so amusing about the case."

"Well, we're *both* working on it— No, wait," she said when he would have interrupted. "I'm just as adamant about proving my innocence as you are about catching the gang of thieves, assuming there is one. Maybe we should work together."

"Ha," he said sarcastically. As if he would be able to think straight when she was near.

There was also the very real possibility of danger if the crooks thought she was leading the cops to them. While she seemed to have faith that the couple would cooperate fully, he didn't have much confidence in the goodness of most people. Life had taught him differently a long time ago. He didn't want Julianne hurt by anyone.

He sighed. How did things get so complicated?

"I have contacts through the clinic and the birthing classes that you don't have," she said in her earnest manner. "You have the resources of the park service and various local law agencies. Doesn't it make sense to combine those?"

"No. You tell me what you find out. I'll do the investigating. That's the way it works."

He noticed the way her lips crimped at the corners with her stubborn look. She shook her head.

"I'm the one who found out where the couple

had gone. You would have sat out there on the desert for hours without finding out they weren't even near there."

"I *did* sit out on the desert for hours," he told her. He swallowed a big gulp of the sangria, but it didn't cool his temper. "Did it ever occur to you that the mother could have been lying? Now she'll warn them, and they really will take off for the high country."

"You don't know that for certain."

He clamped his teeth together. There was no use arguing with her, and he wouldn't bother to do so.

"Give me your glass. I'll refill it."

She took the glass and went inside. He hadn't been aware of drinking it. He decided he'd better watch out or he'd be smashed on the flavorful brew before he realized it.

Following her inside, he was about to tell her to forget it, that he was leaving, when he noticed tears in her eyes, giving them the sheen of molten pewter.

He raked a hand through his hair in frustration. He didn't know how to deal with her, how to keep her out of danger, how to be around her and not want her with everything in him. "Julianne—"

"I'm sorry," she said in a low voice. "I truly am. I just wanted to clear my name and be free of suspicion. I hate people thinking I'm dishonest."

When she tried to smile, her lips trembled.

It was the last straw.

He reached for her. She looked startled, but only

for a moment. Then she raised her hands to his shoulders as he clasped her waist and lifted her to the counter.

Her legs—those strong, slender limbs that he'd dreamed about for a week—pressed against each side of his hips as her arms circled his shoulders. He pressed against the sweet welcoming nook of her body and held her as close as possible, wanting, needing her warmth.

When she lifted her face to his, questions in her eyes that he couldn't answer, he claimed her lips in a kiss he'd experienced in countless ways each night. He felt her hesitation and feared she was going to tell him no. But after a second her arms crept around his neck and she kissed him back.

If the kiss had lasted forever, it wouldn't have been long enough for him.

"I've done this in my dreams a million times this past week," he confided when they came up for air. He kissed along her jaw to her ear. "I've thought of all the things we could do with each other…"

"What?" she murmured, resting her head on his shoulder, her voice sounding as dazed as he felt. "What things?"

"This," he said, running his hands along her body, the tactile sense of her heat penetrating his hands, driving him wild. "And this."

Julianne's lungs quit, simply stopped functioning as his big, gentle hands skimmed over her hips.

When he brought his hands up and cupped her face, she stared at him, unable to hide the fierce need that seemed both foreign and natural to her. With this man the passion felt right, as if it had to be, but odd because she'd never felt this before.

"Julianne," he said in a low growl. The word was a supplication, a blessing, a tormented fact of nature. Tony couldn't stop rubbing his thumbs over her lips. Those soft, enticing lips.

"Kiss me," she demanded. "Kiss me…" Her breath caught in her throat as she was consumed by the blaze of passion in his eyes, the hunger that burned him as much as it did her.

She gasped as he touched the hard, throbbing tips of her breasts, first one, then the other.

"Yes," she cried softly, wanting all of it. "Yes."

"Do you want me?" he demanded, cupping her breasts in his hands and nuzzling them with his mouth.

She made a little humming sound of assent and nipped him on the side of his neck, tiny bites of passion that demanded as much from him as he did from her.

He pressed close and brushed against her again and again. She wrapped her arms around his neck and met his hot, sweet kisses with equal fire.

"I've never experienced this," she told him.

"Tell me what you feel," he said, laying a line of fire across her mouth with his.

"All hot. And confused. Why is it like this? Why with you?"

Their bodies seemed to have developed minds of their own. Their arms meshed, tangled, entwined, bringing them close, then apart—but only a fraction—then melding them into one again. Lips touched lips. Tongues glided against tongues.

The desire she felt was demanding, Julianne thought. Like…like love?

She leaned her head against the cabinet and let him plunder her throat. Plunging her fingers into his thick, dark hair, she closed her eyes and let sensation pour through her, a wild wind of torment and pleasure, and knew it was the part of her that had been missing until now.

"I want more," she said in a barely audible voice. She'd never said anything like that to a man. Biting down on her lower lip, she wondered what had happened to her control and the need to go slowly, to build trust over a long time.

His laughter flowed into her, through her. "There's a lot to share. If we were lovers."

But we're not.

She heard the words he didn't say. They dropped down, down, down inside her to a place that was vast and heavy with sorrow, a place she'd visited only in the distant reaches of childhood and the pain of unbearable loss.

Lifting her head, she met his probing gaze. Neither of them moved for a long time.

"What if we were?" she asked.

He shook his head slightly.

She wasn't sure what that meant. "Where would it go, if we were lovers?"

Dropping his arms, he stepped back, forcing her to release him, too. "Nowhere."

"Because you think I'm a thief?"

His smile was filled with self-mockery. "You can steal my control as fast as any pickpocket can swipe a wallet," he acceded. He rubbed the back of one finger along her cheek. "Passion is natural, but hearts are off-limits."

"I thought they went together."

"Like love and marriage?"

He laughed, and it hurt somewhere deep inside her.

"It isn't in the cards," he said, but in a gentle way, as if he didn't want the words to cause pain. "Not with me."

She pushed his hand aside and jumped down from the counter. "I agree."

He ran a hand through the thick strands of hair that she'd mussed in passionate delight. "So stay out of the way and let me handle the case from now on. I'll call you when I find out anything," he promised. He looked weary.

"Oh? Will they let me take calls from jail?" she asked on an ironic note.

"Don't get smart," Tony ordered, wanting to kiss her again and forcing his gaze from her tempting mouth.

Anger. Passion. Anger again. Theirs was a topsy-turvy relationship at best, he acknowledged. Like her, he'd never had this kind of problem separating business from pleasure in the past. He almost resented her for it.

Except that he wanted her too much.

He headed for the front door and stopped to pull on his shoes. "Don't forget the meeting with the D.A. on Monday."

"It's hard to forget little details like that when one's life hangs in the balance."

"You might go to jail, but you won't hang," he said with a sardonic smile.

"Well, that certainly reassures me." Maintaining her poise, Julianne stood at the door and watched as he left.

Through the gloom of deep twilight, she saw his eyes on her as if intent on memorizing a face on a Wanted poster. He hadn't answered when she'd asked if he still thought she was a thief, she recalled.

She lifted her chin. She would prove her innocence and then she would never have to speak to him again.

Somehow that seemed the worst fate of all.

Chapter Seven

Tony opened one eye and checked the clock. Time to get ready for the cookout over at Diana's place. The afternoon nap hadn't been nearly long enough.

Yawning, he rolled off the sofa and headed for the shower. After doing surveillance last night at the Chaco site, then catching up on paperwork, he really would have preferred to sleep. He was in no mood for a party.

He finished the shower and dressed in dark slacks with a white shirt, the sleeves rolled up. He threw a towel and swimsuit into a small duffel.

He had a reason for going to the get-together. And it wasn't just that Julianne would be there, he sternly reminded the part of him that perked up at the thought.

No, it was the financial wizard he'd met at the council meeting that stirred his interest. Edmund Franks was in a position to know the value of the rare finds at the Chaco digs. Maybe he was also into making some spare change on the side by selling a few.

Shortly before five he left the park service barracks and headed for Diana's condo. He parked under the shade of an imported tree and avoided the sprinklers watering the sweep of lawn in front of the four-building complex. Why did people move to the desert and then try to make it into a tropical paradise?

It was just part of the perverse nature of mankind, he decided. He was frowning over this when he nearly ran into another person who came around a tall bush from a parking area on the other side of the greensward.

"Oh," Julianne said, veering sharply to avoid him.

He caught her arms to steady her and gazed into cool gray eyes that smoldered with anger. Every muscle in his body tightened as her floral fragrance filled his nostrils and her enticing warmth pricked his palms. In an instant he knew the real reason he was here and he was only kidding himself when he denied it.

Because of her. Because she would be here. And where she was, he wanted to be.

Cursing to himself, he put the ridiculous idea— and the sudden longing for something more from life—aside. When she pulled away, he let her go.

She wore a pink knit top over green-striped slacks with pink flowers embroidered at the hem. The polish on her nails matched the pink thongs she wore. With a straw tote and a hat with a floppy brim that hid half her face, she looked chic and oddly unfamiliar.

"I wondered if you would remember Diana's invitation," he said, falling into step beside her.

"Luckily I noticed the date on the calendar this morning, else I would have forgotten."

"Yeah, the weekend has been rather busy," he remarked.

"Don't start," she warned.

Her lips, rosy with an attractive shade of lipstick, thinned to a straight line as she cast him a fulminating glance. "Ah, a woman who holds a grudge," he murmured.

"A person who's trying to clear her name," she retorted, walking faster as if she wanted to get away.

He lengthened his stride. "Which brings a question to mind—how well do you know the financial advisor for the council?"

She slowed down, her brow knit in a thoughtful frown. "I met him when I moved out here last spring. Why?"

She seemed suspicious about his motives and showed some definite attitude where he was concerned. Good. Anger was a contained, understandable emotion. He didn't want anything else from her.

Liar.

He continued doggedly, "He's in a position to know a lot about the Chaco dig and the finds there. Also who in the tribe needs money and that sort of thing."

She stopped abruptly, her eyes going wide as she stared up at him. "I've never thought him to be dishonest, but I suppose he could be."

Tony couldn't help but be amused as her active mind spun off in a dozen directions while she considered the possibilities. He also felt a little relieved when she didn't spring to the other man's defense.

"He always seems to be in on everything, especially if it involves money," she told him, her earlier animosity gone. She laid a hand on his arm. "I can work in some casual questions tomorrow when he starts the audit of the clinic. What should I ask?"

Tony gave her a quelling glare. "Nothing. I'll ask the questions. I just wondered if you thought he was a trustworthy person. You two seemed pretty close when we had lunch last week."

"We're not," she stated. "I, well, we did see each other a few times when I first moved here, but, uh, that didn't work out."

"So you're just friends," he concluded with a sardonic edge. The fact that she and the CPA had dated was nothing to him. Not a thing.

Liar.

"I guess." She wrinkled her brow as if thinking earnestly about the matter. So maybe they weren't the best of pals as it had seemed, at least not on her part.

He stood aside and let her go up the three steps to the condo before him. The oak door was open. A storm door with a screened section allowed them to see inside.

"Hi, you two," Diana called. "Come on in. We're on the back patio."

Looking down the hallway, Tony spotted Diana gesturing for them to join her at the back of the condo. When he and Julianne were on the attractive plant-lined patio, he saw Diana and the other guest give them keen glances.

Edmund's manner seemed relaxed. He stood and gallantly helped Julianne to a chair beside him at the glass-topped patio table. Hiding irritation, Tony sat across from them. Chips and three kinds of salsa were on the table.

"Wine, beer or iced tea?" Diana asked them.

"Tea," he and Julianne said together.

Their eyes met. She immediately looked away while his body gave its usual lurch of attraction.

Chill, he ordered his libido, but without much hope that it actually would. Since tasting Julianne's sweet mouth, his head had been filled with visions of them and all the things they could do together.

"Here you go," Diana said, placing glasses of iced tea on the table. Each glass held a tiny umbrella with a cherry and piece of pineapple stuck on the wooden handle.

"Cheers," Edmund said. His eyes, Tony noted in

annoyance, were on Julianne. The financial advisor
and paralegal were both drinking wine.

Tony ate the fruit and laid the ornament on the
table before taking a long, cool drink. After chatting
for a few minutes, the foursome changed to swimsuits
and headed for the pool. He and Edmund followed
behind the two women along the flagstone path.

Diana was four or five inches taller and was
somewhat curvier than Julianne, who hardly had an
extra ounce of body fat on her. Diana's hair
bounced on her shoulders as she walked. Julianne
had left her hat off, and her hair was braided and
secured to her head.

He thought about removing the pins, one by one,
then had to quickly think of cold things, like ice
floes and snowstorms, to cool his blood.

When he glanced at Edmund, the man was observing Julianne with an expression that Tony
couldn't quite read. Lust? Anger? Both?

He could relate. She drove him crazy, too.

Her legs were perfectly formed with firm,
graceful curves that ended at trim ankles and small
feet. Her one-piece suit was cut high on the legs and
very low in the back. It had a tropical floral design
in bright colors. In contrast, Diana wore a sleek black
number. The two could have easily posed for
swimsuit ads or layouts for romantic getaways on far
islands.

He tore his gaze from the lithe line of Julianne's

back and surveyed the pool area. A couple of families with small kids. Two women reading in lounge chairs. A few others.

Their foursome claimed a table and left their towels and shoes there before diving in. The water was pleasant, and soon four teenagers challenged them to a game of water polo.

Diana accepted. She was a good player. Tony shifted her back into the outdoorsy category. Edmund also proved adept at the game, but it was Julianne who really stood out. She moved through the water with the skill and speed of a sea otter. He suspected growing up with two brothers and a father, who was into physical training, accounted for that.

Tony noted Edmund stayed close to her, their bodies brushing as they both went for the ball. He didn't like the contact. Forcing himself to blunt honesty, Tony wondered if his suspicion of the CPA stemmed from the man's position with the tribal council or his interest in Julianne.

At any rate, his job demanded that he check out everyone who could have access to the artifacts. That included Diana, who was also in a position of trust with tribal members and, like Edmund, knew who was in trouble and needed money.

After thirty minutes, their team was ahead. When he and Julianne dived for the ball at the same time, their legs meshed and only the ball separated them as they went underwater. Their eyes met. An intense shock of desire coursed through Tony.

Pushing away, he let her bring the ball up and put it into play. Edmund served an ace and won the game for them.

Refusing to be drawn into another round of play, the four rinsed off at the outdoor showers and returned to Diana's place. Dressed once more, Tony volunteered to grill the meat while Diana put the rest of the food on the dining room table. By the time he came inside with the platter, the evening was turning cool.

"Tomorrow is your hearing, isn't it?" Edmund asked Julianne during a pause in the replay of the polo game.

Tony was aware of Julianne's gaze on him for a second before she answered. "Yes."

It was obvious she didn't want to discuss the situation. She also didn't mention the meeting he'd set up with the D.A. to go over the evidence.

"Would you like for me to be there?" Edmund asked, his manner overly solicitous.

She shook her head. "I'm sure everything will be fine. At least, my brother, the lawyer, thinks so," she said with droll humor.

Tony frowned at the relief he experienced at her quick rejection of the other man. Other than the case, he had no interest in what she did, or who helped her do it.

Liar.

He ignored the internal voice of his conscience, which showed a tendency to nag of late.

During the course of the evening, he managed to steer the discussion toward the Chaco Canyon discoveries. Neither Diana nor his chief suspect, Edmund, showed undue interest or any detailed knowledge of the artifacts. So the outing was a washout as far as he was concerned.

His gaze went to Julianne and stuck there. She appeared relaxed, but he knew she wasn't. At times she seemed preoccupied and worry flashed into her eyes, then she would laugh at some anecdote—Edmund was full of them and kept the women entertained for most of the evening—and it would be gone.

He felt an overpowering urge to tell her not to worry about the meeting with the D.A. and the possible hearing with the judge afterward. He had a strategy planned out.

If it didn't work and the D.A. insisted on pressing charges against her, then he had the name of a smart local attorney she could call. If he had to testify, he would have to admit she'd brought the stolen goods to the store, but he would also say she obviously didn't know what they were and that her record was spotless.

And that she often did favors for others. Such was her nature, one of kindness and caring, but tough, too, expecting the best of others. The same way his uncle Jeff had treated the orphans in his care, Tony realized.

Odd but he'd thought more of his former home life recently than at any time since he went off to college.

He realized the other three were looking at him. "Sorry," he said, "what was the question?"

Diana repeated it. "We're having cherry pie for dessert. Would you like ice cream with it?"

"Oh, yeah, that would be great."

When ten o'clock rolled around, Julianne rose and thanked Diana for a lovely evening. "I have to open the clinic tomorrow for the audit," she explained with a comical grimace at the CPA.

Edmund also stood. "I'll walk you to your car," he told Julianne. "I have some ideas that may help us locate the couple who gave you the pottery."

Tony perked up at this bit of information. Before he could ask questions, Julianne had answered.

"Really? Any information would be helpful," she said with a grateful smile. "It's very discouraging, I find, to be part of the Most Wanted crowd."

Tony met her sardonic gaze, but he didn't smile at her quip. Actually he felt irritated, as if the other man were interfering with the case. The tumult of emotions from longing to anger confused him. Her smile faltered.

Edmund took her arm before turning to their hostess. "Thanks for having us over. I had a great time." He kissed Diana on the cheek, then escorted Julianne out the door after she said her farewells.

Tony waited until the door was closed behind the couple. "I should be going, too. Tomorrow is a workday. I'm sure you have a full load."

"I'm not tired. Would you like a glass of wine?"

He studied her for a second before nodding. They sat out on the patio after she filled the wine-glasses. "What's your opinion of the financial advisor?" he asked.

"I don't have one. I really don't know him that well. He and Julianne were a couple back in the spring. You should ask her."

"I have," he said. "She doesn't have an opinion, either."

"They're not dating now," she told him. "In case you're interested."

There was a sparkle in her eyes as she added this last phrase. He ignored the gibe. "Julianne and I meet with the district attorney in the morning. I don't have much of a case to lay before him, so I don't think she'll have any trouble, but I'd like to have more info."

"So you're looking for other suspects to tie to the couple other than Julianne?"

"Yeah. It's pretty clear the couple used her trust in them to get her to deliver the pots. Somehow they learned she walked into a sting operation and left the area before I got out there. I want to know who warned them."

"Hmm, Edmund knows everything the council knows. He's been helping them with finances for over two years. They seem to depend on his advice."

"Two years. That was before the pots started disappearing and around the time they found the new site."

Diana shrugged. "I haven't seen or heard anything about him that's bad. Actually, I think he's quite nice."

Tony noted the defensive note. He finished off the wine and stood. "Well, I'd better be going, too. If you think of anything…" He paused. "Do you have client-attorney-type privilege with the cases you look into?"

"Absolutely."

"Okay, outside of that, if you see anything you think is suspicious, would you let me know?"

"Of course." Her manner seemed completely open and friendly as she walked him to the door.

"It was a great evening," he remembered to say before he left.

"Thanks. I enjoyed it, too."

At the barracks, he recalled the defensive note when his hostess had spoken up for Edmund. If she was interested in the CPA and he was interested in Julianne, that could lead to complications.

As if he didn't already have plenty of those.

He tried to figure out all the possible motives of everyone close to the case and if anyone would have cause to frame Julianne. Was his own judgment being warped by the depth of the attraction he felt toward Julianne?

Giving a low curse, he reminded himself he was on an important case. That was his first concern at the moment. A personal life came a distant second.

Actually, it came dead last.

When he slipped into bed, a heavy sigh escaped him. He wondered if Julianne was also in bed...and if she was thinking of him and the blood-stirring kisses they'd shared. He couldn't seem to get them out of his mind for any length of time.

Julianne went to the clinic shortly after seven on Monday morning. It wasn't open yet, so she had some time to herself. Edmund had told her he would be there at eight.

She made sure the ledgers in the computer program were up to date as of the prior Friday. With no clerical help, she and the other nurses had to keep up with the finances and the patients' files, too. She wanted to be especially careful to stay on top of things so no one could find fault with her record keeping.

The black fog hanging over her spirits thickened. Last night, after going to bed, she'd wondered how long Tony had stayed at Diana's. She'd also realized she was jealous. That had been a stunning revelation.

However, if he was interested in Diana, then how did either of them explain the kisses they had shared, the hunger that stirred them both when they were together?

And why, why, *why* did she want more from him

when she, the most cautious virgin in the state, as her best friend had once teased, had never gone that far with any man?

Putting the distressing thoughts aside, she checked over the office and decided she was as ready for the audit as she would ever be.

Exactly at eight, Edmund tapped on the door.

"Hi," she said when she let him in.

"Good morning. Wow, you look beautiful," he said with an approving smile.

She wore a simple dress of hunter-green with a matching jacket trimmed in ecru lace. Gold earrings and taupe shoes and purse completed the outfit. Her heart thumped nervously at the thought of facing the district attorney and proclaiming her innocence or whatever one did.

"Tony and I are meeting with the D.A. today," she explained.

"Do you have an attorney?"

She shook her head. "Unless you count my brother. He says there's no real evidence against me."

"Ancient artifacts aren't evidence?"

She cast him a worried glance. "Do you think the judge will believe I didn't know they were stolen?"

He took her hand and laid his other hand over it, stroking lightly along the back. "I'm sure he will. If Chief Windover's word isn't good enough, I have the report on you that I did for the council before you were hired. Your professional reputation is spotless."

Her mouth dropped open. "*You* investigated me?"

"Checked on your credentials and references," he explained. "I can vouch for your sterling character."

His manner seemed sincere, but there was something about him that she didn't quite trust. He was just too…too helpful.

She removed her hand from his grasp. "Thank you. I'll let you know if you need to slip me a file so I can hack my way out of prison." She managed a smile.

He chuckled, then gestured toward the desk. "Show me where you keep your records."

Thirty minutes later she left him randomly pulling records and comparing them to the computer charts.

Julianne was parked in front of the D.A.'s office when Tony arrived. He joined her on the sidewalk in front of the old limestone-and-brick building where justice had been meted out for well over a hundred years.

He sucked in a harsh breath as he checked her over. She was beautiful in her green outfit. A pleasurable jolt spun through him as images of Julianne in his arms bloomed in his mind.

He held them at bay. Today was serious business, and he had to keep his wits about him.

The smile she turned on him was stoic and

reserved, as if she was determined to remain calm at all costs. He could identify with that.

"Good morning," she said.

"Hi." He led the way inside. Outside a lighted door, he paused. "Don't be nervous."

She managed a brief laugh. "Let's see, I'm being audited at the clinic, we're meeting with the district attorney about a crime I know nothing about, but can't prove. You're right. What's there to be nervous about?"

"Let me do the talking." He tried to be reassuring as he held the door open. "I assume your brother got hold of a local attorney for you. Will he be here?"

"I didn't call anyone. Cal said you had no real case against me, so I thought—" She shrugged to indicate she didn't know what she'd thought.

Tony shook his head as they started down the long corridor of the courthouse. He knocked, then opened a door marked No Admittance and gestured to her to go inside when a deep voice told them to come in.

The district attorney sat at his desk. He didn't stand to greet them.

Tony introduced himself and the suspect to Charles Patterson. "Thanks for meeting with us," he added.

The D.A. was tall, overweight by a hundred pounds and had crinkles at the corners of his eyes as if he either smiled or squinted a lot. Tony had asked some of his contacts about the man.

A consummate politician, Patterson had ambitions for higher office, the head ranger at the Chaco dig had said. "Be careful," Dick Worth had warned. "You don't want to get on his bad side."

Tony wasn't inclined to kowtow to anyone, but he plastered on a smile and leaned across the desk to shake hands with the man.

"To what do I owe the pleasure of this visit?" the D.A. asked.

He and Julianne looked at Tony.

Tony quickly laid out the facts of the case, including her part. "My investigation leads me to conclude she was just the messenger, doing a favor for the couple. She's been cooperative in trying to locate them."

"She also brought the artifacts in and was going to take money for them," the D.A. reminded him.

Tony shrugged. "Out here, people do things for each other, like drive a hundred miles out of their way to give someone a ride to a relative's funeral or ask someone who's already going to town to do them a favor."

"Is that your story, that you were merely helping out a friend?" Patterson asked Julianne.

Julianne nodded. "I'd seen Josiah's pottery work. I watched him make a vase a few months ago. I had no reason to think the pots weren't his."

"There are articles in the newspaper all the time about thefts of native artifacts," the D.A. mentioned.

His eyes narrowed. "Didn't you become suspicious when you saw the pottery?"

She shook her head. "I didn't even look at it. Josiah put the box in the back of my car. I didn't take it out until two days later when I went to the store."

"Her fingerprints weren't on the pottery," Tony said. "We only found one set, those belonging to Josiah."

The D.A. frowned. "I don't think we can let a case of this magnitude drop. Dr. Jones over at the museum said those vases were priceless. How much was she going to take for them?"

"A thousand dollars," Tony admitted. Sensing refusal in the attorney, he added, "The council had her investigated thoroughly before they hired her to run the clinic and health services. Chief Windover has indicated he will personally vouch for her. From my own investigation, she was an honor student all through school and hasn't had so much as a parking ticket in her life."

He met the narrowed gaze of the district attorney and witnessed a cold, calculating anger there. The man wanted to pin the rap on somebody and didn't care who it was as long as he got a conviction. For a second, Tony felt as if he were being judged and found guilty of some crime.

Like lusting after the suspect?

Setting his jaw, he kept a poker face and didn't back down from the other man's glare. "Other than the delivery of the goods, which ties in with other charitable acts by the suspect, there're no links between her and those who have worked the Chaco dig. She arrived in town last January. There were thefts before that time. With the tribal council speaking in her defense and no other findings against her, it would be difficult to prove Ms. Martin knew what she was doing."

Tony could almost see the wheels turning in the political mind behind the cool stare the district attorney turned on him. When the man finally nodded, Tony knew he'd made his point.

"I'll call the court clerk and cancel the hearing," Patterson said, making up his mind. He turned to Julianne. "If you learn anything, you're to let this office know immediately."

It was a threat, and Tony didn't like it. Before Julianne could speak, he said, "She will. She's done all she could to cooperate with me and the officers working on the case. As my report stated, the couple fled. Until we contact them and find out how they acquired the pottery, we have nothing to go on."

"Will the investigation take a back burner now?"

Tony shook his head. "It's my number-one priority. In fact, I'm staking out the dig site at night."

"That's good. The media always has a lot to say when we fail to solve important cases like this." He nodded as if satisfied that Tony would stay on top of it.

"I'm glad that's over," Tony muttered, walking down the hallway at a fast clip. "The man's a shark. Dick warned me the D.A. was out to make a name for himself."

On the courthouse steps, Julianne dug in her heels and refused to take another step. "You've been investigating my background all this time without saying a word to me," she accused.

"That's right." He took her arm and urged her toward their parked vehicles.

She stopped beside her car. "That is just despicable. Who all did you contact behind my back?"

"Your high school and college, the references you gave the council." He returned her glare. "It's my job. That's what an investigator does."

She yanked open the car door so that he had to step back or get slammed in the chest. "You could have told me."

He heaved a sigh. "No officer of the law tells a suspect what he's doing. Ask your brother. He'll explain it to you in simple terms."

She glowered at him and cranked the engine.

Angrier than he'd been since…since the last time they'd quarreled, he stalked to his SUV and drove off without looking back.

Women, he thought. Did Julianne appreciate what he'd done for her? Did she thank him for putting his own reputation on the line to defend her?

No.

Did she understand that a man had to do his job and maintain a proper distance when they were involved on more than one level?

No.

Besides, they weren't involved, not on any level. At least, not on any that counted.

Anyway he wasn't going to think about her or the problems associated with her anymore.

And that was final, no matter how fresh and lovely she'd looked in her outfit that morning, no matter how sweetly she'd filled his nights with impossible dreams and his days with yearning for things that could never be. Not for him.

Arriving at the empty barracks he currently called home, he began to wonder if a person ever got over having that restless spirit.

Chapter Eight

Julianne held well-baby morning on Tuesday and well-mother afternoon on Wednesday. During these hours she had one of the practical nurses weigh the patients and take their vitals to see that all was going to plan.

If anyone had questions the LPN couldn't answer or there were indications of illness, the nurse sent them to her. On Wednesday, it seemed every patient had problems. It was after seven that evening before she locked up and left the clinic.

Upon arriving at the cottage, she changed clothes and walked briskly along the rim of the arroyo for thirty minutes to unwind.

However, today the effort mostly shifted her worries from professional to personal ones. While no charges or threats of prison loomed over her head at present, she couldn't help but dwell on the thefts of ancient goods.

And that rumination brought her to Special Investigator Aquilon. Whatever his personal opinion, Tony had gone to bat for her with the district attorney. *After* checking her background thoroughly.

Okay, that was his job, as he'd often pointed out to her while in his exasperated mode. She had to smile at recalling their quarrels, but immediately became serious again. She'd been ungracious to him, unable to get past her alarmed anger over possibly being indicted for grand theft due to her own ignorance. She owed him for his help.

Back at the house, she showered and slipped into a clean T-shirt and jeans. After preparing three chicken salad sandwiches, she packed them and a bag of baby carrots into a small cooler. A package of cookies, cold bottles of iced tea and a thermos of coffee—to help keep him awake during his vigil— completed the meal. She headed for Chaco Canyon shortly before nine and arrived an hour later.

She stopped at the artifact trailer. No one was there.

Going on down the bumpy road, she came to the cottonwood where Tony had parked on their previous visit. She stopped beside it and got out, holding the basket protectively in front of her.

The hair on her nape rose as a gust of wind ruffled her bangs. Silence surrounded her except for the slight murmuring of running water from some unseen spring in the cliff face. She turned toward the sound.

Again she felt a strong presence, as if the people from long ago still roamed the canyon.

"What are you doing here?" a familiar voice asked.

The softness of it was more startling than a shout. She turned to find Tony standing only a few feet from her.

"Where did you come from?" she demanded in a whisper, unable to think clearly as fear and excitement rushed madly through her, making her tremble.

"I was over at the new dig when I saw lights flash along the canyon wall. I thought it might be—"

When he stopped abruptly, she finished the thought for him. "The thieves coming for more goods?"

Moon glow barely reflected from his face and the whites of his eyes. His shrug was a movement of shadow against shadow, barely visible. She realized he was dressed totally in black.

"Why are you here?" he asked in a repressive manner that said she shouldn't have come.

"I remembered what you told the D.A. about staking out the place at night. I wanted to…to thank you for your help with him. I think he would have put me in jail and thrown away the key." Her laughter sounded forced.

He studied her without saying a word.

She indicated the basket. "I hadn't had dinner, I thought about you being out here all night, so I fixed something for the two of us."

"You're just full of kind acts," he muttered.

Her heart lacerated by the scornful words, she turned toward her car and prepared to retreat with as much dignity as she could muster. "Well, you're obviously not hungry."

"I am."

His voice was deep, husky and…not angry…but tense with other emotions. She held his harsh stare for endless moments and waited.

"My truck's this way," he said.

He took the basket and walked past the trees. In an outcropping of limestone beyond the trailer, in a place too rocky for any vehicle to traverse—or so she would have thought—the black SUV suddenly loomed in front of them.

He opened the passenger door for her—no inside light came on—silently latched it when she was inside and joined her after scanning the area.

Julianne, her eyes adjusting to the darkness, also took in the awesome span of the canyon from this vantage point. Other than an occasional gust of wind, as if the world breathed in well-paced gasps, the narrow valley remained eerily silent.

"It's so quiet," she said, again in a whisper.

"A couple of coyotes came through after the park

ranger went off duty," he said. "That's about all the action I've seen tonight."

She gave him his share of the food she'd brought. He ate quickly, his attention focused beyond the windows, his gaze moving restlessly from one shadow to the next. She observed him as intently as he did the landscape.

The inside of the SUV was warm. The simple food was comforting. His masculine presence flowed over and around her, wrapping her in the safety of his protective nature.

When she sighed in contentment, he turned to her.

She swallowed the last of her meal with a gulp of iced tea. Her throat had a tendency to close when he studied her in that piercing manner.

"I brought some coffee, too," she said. "I thought you might need it later."

"I might," he agreed in a strangely tight voice that ruffled any composure that had survived his stare. An awkward silence passed between them.

Julianne took a deep breath. "Well, I should go."

"Yeah. You should."

She made no move to leave. He made no move to assist her departure.

He tossed their sandwich wrappings into the basket and lifted it over the seat into the back. When he slid closer, her eyes widened.

"Why?" he asked, placing a crooked finger under

her chin and lifting her face to his as he lowered his head. "Why can't I resist you?"

"I don't know." Waves of confusion, anticipation and other emotions too fleeting to read washed over her. "I've never felt like this, either."

His chuckle was wry, but reassuring. "Well, I asked," he said, as if to himself, and brought his head an inch closer.

She waited, wanting to reach for him, to take what the passion demanded. But one part, the part of her that was always cautious, hesitated, not sure if this was meant to be. The moment remained suspended for a breathless eternity as they looked deep into each other's eyes.

"Julianne," he whispered just as their lips met in a fiery melding of passion.

She heard surrender in the word, and something else. Loneliness, she thought, and wanted to comfort him, to tell him she would hold him forever.

The kiss was everything she'd ever dreamed of. A sweet exploration of the depths of the passion between them. An expression of needs that only the other could fulfill. A hesitation and a hunger, in equal parts, as their mouths blended and their hearts beat in unison.

When she laid her hand against his chest, she sensed his strength and the gentleness within him. Both spoke to her in a way that was new and deeply felt.

Because of this man. This man and no other.

His hands roamed over her back, under her shirt.

She gave a little gasp when he caressed her bare skin. She hadn't bothered with a bra. When he discovered that fact, he paused, then touched her breasts as he had once before. He stroked the hard tips and cupped their weight in his palms until she gasped with delight.

"I've waited for this," he whispered, branding an imprint of kisses along her jaw. "I've dreamed about us, about being with you. I've wanted it."

"It's a strange wanting," she told him, running her fingers through his hair and stroking his neck. "Scary in a way. I don't understand it."

When she slid her arms around his neck, he lifted her so he could scoot to her side of the seat. She curled up against him in an instinctive manner, wanting, needing this closeness in her soul.

Their hearts pounded in unison. She tried to quiet the rush of blood through her brain so she could think, but it felt so good here in his arms, so right. She wished she could grasp the moment forever and not have to think beyond it.

He laid her back against his arm, pushed her T-shirt out of the way and bent his head. When he took her nipple into his mouth, it sent a shaft of electricity through her so strong it was almost painful.

Tremors ran over her. Old fear battled with new longings. She couldn't stop shaking.

Tony felt the trembling in Julianne's slender body. He recognized the passion, but the fear he sensed surprised him. With absolute certainty, he understood two things—that she was inexperienced in passion and that she wasn't ready for greater intimacy at this moment.

After tucking her T-shirt into place and linking his hands together at her waist, he simply held her while the trembling slowly abated. He kissed the top of her head, her temples, her nose, but nothing more intimate than that.

Julianne lifted her head and stared at him in the faint light of the rising moon. There was no demand in the look he gave her, only patient control that she found reassuring.

He kissed her on the mouth, but the heat was subdued. She realized he wasn't going to push past her barriers, but did he feel cheated that she was holding out on him after going so far?

Emotions whirling, she whispered, "I'm…I'm sorry. I didn't meant to, to—"

"It's okay," he told her. "We don't have to go further than this. Kissing is very nice. Very, very nice."

His chuckle was reassuring.

When he kissed her once more, it was passionate but not so hot as before. She kissed him back, realizing that she no longer had to be afraid of being pushed for more than she wanted to give. There was a certain type of freedom in that, she found. She could touch him without worrying about where it would lead and whether she wanted to follow.

Slipping her hands under his sweatshirt, she went on her own trek of discovery. She brushed her fingers through the light patch of hair on his chest, rubbed down his sides and over his back. She was acutely aware of his arousal, but it didn't worry her or make her draw away as she would have in the past.

When she touched the prominent ridge, he quickly but gently removed her hand. "You're not ready to go there," he whispered as he planted kisses along her jaw line. "And I won't. Not tonight."

Just when she thought she might be getting an insight into him and his patience with her reticence, a voice squawked from the dashboard, "Tony, got something interesting for you." She nearly jumped out of her skin.

Tony reached over and pushed a button. "Right, Chuck, go ahead."

"We caught a guy coming from your way in a pickup. He has a few shards with him, but nothing complete. I'm taking him to the station. You might want to interrogate him right away before someone from the D.A.'s office does."

"Why? What's he saying?"

"That he'd come to town to see a local nurse about some antiques she wanted to sell and that they'd made contact over the Internet."

Tony muttered a curse, then hit the button again. "I'll be in ASAP." They signed off.

Even in the dim light, Julianne could see the hard

line of his jaw. "He can't be talking about me," she said. "I don't have any antiques."

He nodded as he slid her off his lap and took his place behind the wheel. "I should have been patrolling the area as I usually do. I might have caught him at the site." His tone was one of grim anger, directed at himself.

Worry ate at her. Even if Tony believed she had nothing to do with the interloper, she was still the distraction that had caused him to forget his duty, and he was obviously upset with himself over it.

"I'll drop you by your car," he said.

She remained silent while he backed down the slope and turned the SUV. At her compact, he grabbed the picnic basket, put it in the back of her car and made sure she was inside with the doors locked before stepping back.

"Go home. Don't stop for anything, not even someone trying to wave you down on the road." He hesitated, then added, "Thanks for dinner."

"You're welcome." She waited for him to tell her he would call her tomorrow, or stop by, but he hurried away without saying more. He had obligations and another suspect to investigate. And he certainly did a thorough job of that.

Mulling over the past hour, she put her vehicle into gear and followed him down the gravel road, but at a much slower pace. At her house, preparing for bed, she admitted there was an ache inside her that had nothing to do with fear from the past and everything to do with the man who made her feel attractive, desirable and safe in his arms.

It wasn't a total shock to realize she'd wanted more from him, more than she'd ever wanted from a man. What was odd about it was the fact that she hadn't known him forever.

But then, she thought as confusion rose again, she hadn't fallen for any of the friends from her childhood, either. So…so maybe trust wasn't built on the length of time she'd known the person?

Julianne got a call the next morning just as she was getting ready to leave for the clinic, an hour before opening time as usual. "Hello?" she said, unable to disguise the lilt in her voice. She was sure it was Tony.

It was.

"Can you come down to the station before you go to work?" he asked.

Her smile dimmed a bit. "Yes. Why?"

"We need to know if you can identify the man Chuck apprehended last night."

"Oh. I was just going out the door. I'll be there in five minutes."

After they hung up, she grabbed her purse and headed for the car, a tiny worry nagging at her. He didn't sound happy to hear her voice. In fact, there was definitely a note of caution present.

There were probably other people around, so naturally he couldn't say anything personal. Reassured, she drove to town and the station that served the area. Tony's SUV was there. She parked next to it and went inside, her heart skipping every now and then.

The sergeant who'd fingerprinted her nearly two weeks ago greeted her at the front desk. He directed her down a short hallway and into a room to her left. The door was open and Tony and Chuck were in the room when she peeked in.

Chuck spotted her. "Come in," he said, giving her a friendly smile. "Good to see you again."

"Thanks. You, too," she said. "I think."

Tony gave her a solemn nod and a brief smile, if one could call the slight curving of his attractive mouth a smile. He looked tired, as if he'd been up all night, but he'd changed to fresh clothing at some point. He seemed unfamiliar in slacks, a white shirt with a tie and dress shoes. He looked like a man who meant business.

"What am I supposed to do?" she asked him.

"Just look at the guy in the next room when they bring him in." He closed the door to their room before speaking into a phone. "Okay, you're clear to bring in the suspect."

"What is his name?"

"Doug Lovelace. He's from Nevada. The address on his driver's license checks out. Here they come."

The three of them gathered in front of the one-way mirror as another officer ushered a man into the interrogation room. He looked to be in his mid-thirties and had longish hair, an unkempt beard and wore jeans and a stained blue work shirt over a T-shirt.

Tony motioned toward the mirror. "Do you know him?"

Julianne shook her head. "I don't recall ever seeing him before." She turned to Chuck. "He said a *nurse* was going to sell him antiques?"

Chuck nodded.

"Did he have my name?"

Chuck hesitated.

Tony answered. "Julie somebody. He said he didn't have a last name, but she was a nurse. He was supposed to meet her in town, but she never showed up."

"Well, I know I've never spoken with him, much less offered to sell him anything." She sighed in disgust.

Tony spoke into a speaker connected to the next room. "Okay, you can take him back to the cell."

"I want to see a lawyer," the man yelled toward the window. "I didn't do anything wrong. This is a mistake, a big mistake."

After he was led away, Julianne glanced at Tony with a rueful smile. "Where have I heard that expression before?"

He didn't share her wry amusement. "You're sure

you've never seen him? He never stopped at the clinic needing medical treatment or something?"

"No, never. I would remember if he had." A tiny chill of alarm swept down her back at his questions. No warmth from the moments they had shared last night lingered in his eyes. They could have been strangers.

"Okay, you're free to go," he said in an official tone.

Julianne exhaled loudly. "This may be paranoid, but I'm beginning to feel somebody out there doesn't like me."

Only she and Chuck laughed.

She checked her watch. "Well, I'd better get to work."

Chuck glanced at her, then Tony. "Me, too. I have a couple of calls to make." He left the room, closing the door behind him.

"We all have work to do," Tony said, going to the door and opening it with an impatient yank. "Thank you for coming in," he said formally.

Her mouth went dry. She'd heard friends complain that men often withdrew just when they were beginning to get close. Was Tony's manner an example of that behavior? Or did he think...surely he didn't think...

"You don't really think I know anything about this man, do you?" she asked, puzzled by his manner.

"No, I don't."

"Oh." The arguments she'd mustered in defense died on her tongue.

"I have things to do," he said abruptly and left her standing in the little room alone and bewildered.

She swallowed the knot in her throat and headed for work. Apparently Tony had decided the previous night had been a serious mistake on his part. She got the picture. This was business, and pleasure had no place here. Setting a smile in place, she left the building, fervently hoping her encounters with cops and jails were at an end.

Chapter Nine

Julianne waved at Diana and picked her way through the lunch crowd to the table where her friend waited.

"So, how did things go for you this week?" Diana asked with a knowing smile. "I understand there was some excitement at Chaco Canyon, something involving you and Tony?"

This wasn't a subject Julianne wanted to discuss, but she nodded pleasantly. She quickly explained about Tony coming to her defense with the D.A. and her repaying him with the impromptu picnic. She told Diana about Chuck catching a thief heading cross-country from the canyon site and once again, being implicated in the artifact scheme. "I don't understand any of this."

Like Julianne, Diana was chagrined that people would steal the ancient finds. She was also indignant on her friend's behalf. "Had you ever heard of the guy?"

"No. I had to go to the jail yesterday and see if I could identify him, but it was no one I knew."

"Surely no one believed his story," Diana said.

"No, but it's a frustrating development."

After they ordered, Julianne determinedly turned the discussion to other topics. There was no point in hashing over her problems the whole time.

However, while they chatted about work and how the week had gone, Julianne kept thinking of Wednesday night and the kisses she and Tony had shared, those magical moments when the earth had disappeared and there were just the two of them on that lovely cloud of passion. Had he really been busy with his investigation since then, or was he avoiding her?

"Oh, look," Diana said. "There's Tony. Over here," Diana called, half standing and waving across the room.

Julianne groaned silently. She wasn't ready for this, but it was too late. Tony spotted them and headed their way.

"Hi," Diana said, giving him a delighted smile when he stopped beside the table and greeted them.

Julianne nodded. She couldn't have smiled if someone had held a gun to her head and ordered it.

"Won't you join us?" Diana, ever the gracious hostess, asked him while Julianne prayed he wouldn't.

"I've eaten." He turned to Julianne. "I need you to come with me."

Her heart gave a gigantic lurch. "Wh-why?" She hated the little stutter.

"I think I've found the couple who gave you the pottery. I need you to identify them."

"Are they at the police station?"

"No, over in Arizona. I followed them from here to a place near the Hubbell Trading Post."

"That's wonderful." Diana turned to Julianne. "They can clear your name, and you can put all this behind you."

The waitress arrived with their salads and plump rolls glistening with butter.

"I haven't eaten," she told Tony, as if that meant she couldn't possibly go with him.

He pulled out a chair. "I'll wait." He ordered a cup of coffee and the cherry pie special.

Julianne experienced a dispiriting sense of déjà vu on the trip. Although they were off I-40 and on Highway 63 in Arizona, the silent, uneasy atmosphere was exactly like the trip back to Chaco Canyon the other night so she could get her car.

"Yeah," he said, "me, too."

"What?"

"You sighed."

"Oh." She clenched her hands, realized what she was doing and forced her fingers to relax. She sighed again.

"I suppose we had better talk about it," he said.

"About Wednesday night?"

"Yes."

"Well, the first part was great—"

He threw on the brakes, turned onto a dirt pullout well off the main road and came to a dusty, sliding stop. "Are you trying to make me have a wreck?" he demanded.

She shook her head.

He crossed his arms on the steering wheel and rested his forehead on them. He sighed, so wearily that the hard anger inside her dissipated somewhat.

She continued on a soft note, "It was yesterday morning that upset me. You were cold and distant, as if you'd never seen me before. I didn't like that." Silence prevailed for a painful thirty seconds.

"What was I supposed to do—grab you and kiss you senseless when you walked in the door?" he demanded, thrusting a hand through his hair and staring at her in frustration. And hunger.

Her heart kicked up its beat to frantic. She couldn't bring herself to ask him why he hadn't called or stopped by last night. "Have you investigated the man Chuck arrested?"

"Lovelace. Yeah. He has some priors in Nevada, and the cops there said he's a known liar and opportunist."

"Then why did you act as if you thought I could be guilty?"

"I never thought that. I didn't mean to give you that impression."

"Well, you did. Why?"

"Because we needed some distance." He glanced at her, then stared at the huge rock formation.

"*You* needed distance. I'm fine."

Tony was silent for a moment. "The men in my family aren't good prospects," he said finally, his face grim and earnest.

She thought of her childhood home, of the things they did as a family before her mom's brutal death, of the fun they had. "I don't recall the subject coming up," she said in dogged denial of her heart's yearning.

A muscle in his jaw clenched. Emotions too swift to read flicked through the dark depths of his eyes.

"My father walked out when I was three, shortly after Krista, my sister, was born," he told her. "My mom remarried, but my stepfather couldn't seem to settle in one place, either. Restless spirits, my mother called them. She divorced my stepdad after ten years of following the rodeo circuit."

"So then you stayed in one place?"

His expression changed to one of bitterness that

caused an ache in her heart. She wanted to pull him into her arms and hold him, just hold him. She didn't move.

"A funny thing happened," he said with no emotion and no sign of humor. "Both my stepfather and my mother were killed within a few months of each other. He was in an auto accident. She was fatally wounded by a neighbor who got into an argument with a friend over a game of cards."

"Oh, Tony," she murmured and blinked hard against the tears that formed for that boy and his sister.

He glanced at her, his gaze opaque, his thoughts closed. "We survived, Krista and I."

"What happened after that? Where did you go?"

"We lived with my stepuncle until social services stepped in, decided we didn't belong with Uncle Jeff and sent us to a foster home. The foster father used to whip us with a belt when he got mad."

Julianne was at once furious on his behalf. "How horrible. Did you report him?"

"We ran away and went to our stepcousin, Jeremy. The three of us hid out in the hills." His sudden smile had a feral quality. "It was over a year before we were caught."

"It must have been a terrible time."

"Not really. The three of us had each other." He shook his head slightly. "It doesn't matter. That was years in the past. We're all fine now."

"What happened after you were found?"

"Jeremy's uncle took us in. Again. Uncle Jeff was a brother of my stepfather. He adjusted his life so that the welfare people would let us live with him and Jeremy."

"He must be a wonderful person," she said softly, hearing the love and respect in Tony's voice.

"The best. He was an Army Ranger who had his foot blown off during the Gulf War, but he never complained. He taught by example and talked to us kids as if we were real people."

She liked the gentleness on his face when he spoke, and the way his eyes crinkled at the corners when he smiled as memories of the past evidently flicked through his mind.

"I think you're a lot more like your uncle Jeff than you realize."

He gave her a startled glance, as if this idea had never occurred to him, then shook his head as if to clear it of the thoughts her statement inspired.

"Yeah, right. Now that we have that behind us, if we could proceed on the quest to find the suspect, I would appreciate it," he said in a hard voice.

She gave him a mock frown, then grinned. "I'm not the one who came to a screeching halt and brought the Wednesday-night interlude up," she reminded him.

Instead of leaving, he turned on her, clasped her shoulders and took the "oh" from her startled lips in a searing kiss whose purpose was, she suspected, to shut her up and vent his frustration.

She didn't move her arms, but she did give herself to the caress. Opening her mouth, she stroked his hard lips with her tongue. This time he was the one who jerked.

He pulled back and glared at her.

She gave him a sweet smile.

When he groaned and reached for her, she leaned as far into him as the seat belt permitted and gave him kiss for kiss. Soon the heat in the SUV went to the sizzling point.

"I could take you right here," he muttered, his tone stern but his hands gentle as he cupped her breasts and stroked the tips. "I want to. How I want to."

They kissed again, using their hands in the foreplay this time. As they came up for air once more, a passing driver sat on his horn. His passengers waved when Tony and she looked around.

"Damn," Tony said, running a hand through his hair when she leaned back into her seat. He put the SUV in gear, eased the gas pedal down and guided the vehicle back onto the road. "That was probably the only car in forty miles. Good thing he came along."

Julianne didn't think it was so great, but she kept the thought to herself. "Don't vent your frustrations on me in the future," she advised.

There was a moment of tense silence, then he surprised her by smiling, sardonically, yes, but a smile. "Oh, is that what we were doing?"

She didn't bother to answer.

Thirty minutes later he took a gravel highway to the east shortly after passing the historic trading post. Upon traveling beside a wash for twenty minutes, they arrived at a tiny lake where several families were camping.

"There," Tony said, "those two with the baby. Is that the couple who gave you the pottery?"

She recognized the ones he pointed out. Disappointed, she shook her head. "I did help them with the birth of their baby, but that isn't Josiah and his family."

"He looks like the mug shot."

"That photo was taken when he was a teenager. He's gained weight since then. That man isn't Josiah."

"I spotted them coming from the direction of his mother's house. I was positive he was the one."

"You were wrong." She met his gaze and realized there was speculation in his eyes. "What?"

"You wouldn't protect them because you feel sorry for his little family, would you?"

She considered, then shook her head. "I'm not that forgiving. When people involve others in their misdeeds, they violate trust and friendship."

He nodded. On the drive back to Gallup, they stopped once for gas. He bought them each a soda. Conversation was sparse on the nearly two-hour trip. Dark clouds gathered, the wind whipped up and rain hit the windshield on the road to her house. Hail mixed with the rain.

The cottage looked blessedly normal when they arrived, her car safely under the carport where she'd left it, the bird-of-paradise bush flat-topped by the storm winds.

"Well, thanks for an interesting trip," she said, preparing to make a dash for the house.

"Julianne," he said.

A shiver went down her spine. "Yes?"

"Did I violate your trust?" he asked on a strained note, his gaze dark and oddly haunted.

She hadn't realized the depths of his personal integrity until now. His question made her want to lean into his strong embrace and stay there. "No. What happened between us happened because we both wanted it." She paused. "I was an active participant."

His eyes seemed to smolder at her words and the light laugh she managed at the admission.

"That was a lapse on my part. I almost missed the looting of the site while we…while I was otherwise occupied."

A heaviness fell over her. He blamed himself, but she knew she was the distraction that had caused the inattention to duty. "Well, tomorrow is a new day. Surely something will happen now that you have a suspect in hand. Maybe he was working with someone local."

"Right," he murmured on the same note of irony she'd used. He smiled at her, a true smile, as she jumped from the car and dashed through the rain to her house.

Once inside she dried her face on her sleeve and watched his truck disappear into the storm.

The pitfalls of paradise, she thought, recalling their kisses. Having tasted that delicious fruit once, it was difficult not to want it again and again.

But not just with any man, only with the right one. The perfect one, the one for her.

And that one, she realized, was Tony Aquilon.

She closed her eyes, but the truth lingered. Julianne Martin, the most cautious virgin in the state, was in love.

"The trailer was broken into," Bruce Jones said with a worried frown on his handsome face. "Luckily, we didn't have much in it, but the new piece of pottery is gone, the one that only had a chip out of the bottom."

"That was our best piece from the new level," Tony said. He stood and gazed out the window at the dark clouds hanging over the canyon.

The wind whipped the tops of the cottonwoods along the canyon, but no rain had fallen. He felt as dispirited as the weather promised to be before the day was over. He wished the Saturday-afternoon meeting with Dr. Bruce Jones and Dick Worth, the park manager, was over.

Dick cleared his throat and leaned back in the

rickety chair behind his desk. "The council sent over a guard for the weekend," he told them. "They're worried about these constant raids on the old settlements."

"I'd offer to help, but with classes at the university and trying to get the artifacts cataloged, as well as supervising the students who're doing the volunteer work, I don't have a spare minute."

"We realize that," Dick assured the other man.

Tony realized the park manager was pale and drawn. Dark bags underlined his eyes. There was a dejected weariness about the older man that indicated a sleepless night.

He could identify with that. Wednesday night he'd been preoccupied with Julianne, then with apprehending the thief.

Thursday and Friday nights his problems had been of a different nature. With one of the park rangers taking over guard duty, he'd been able to sleep in his own bed…or at least make the attempt.

Ha.

All he'd done was think of Julianne and how she'd felt in his arms, how she'd responded to his touch, followed his every lead. How much he wanted her…

"What do you think?" Dick asked.

Tony gave him a blank stare.

"About finishing up the dig and backfilling the site earlier than planned?"

"I think there's older stuff below the new level," Tony said, turning back to the room and tucking his thumbs in his front pockets. "I'd hate not to find evidence of the very first settlement if it's there."

"That would go nicely in your dissertation, wouldn't it?" Bruce asked.

Tony took umbrage at the tone, but suppressed the feeling. He shrugged. "I really haven't had time to think that far ahead, I'm afraid." He glanced at the sky again. "Since the site is covered for the weekend, I think I'll head for home before the storm breaks."

Dick chuckled. "Get your rest, son. I'll be in the area most of tomorrow. We have the sites covered at night, so all should be well."

Given the man's history of high blood pressure and the heart attack, Tony considered returning the park manager's advice about getting enough rest, but he knew neither of them would heed the recommendation if duty called.

Thunder rumbled over Standing Rock as Tony headed back to town. He flicked on the radio to catch a weather report. Flash-flood warnings were being broadcast across the state well before the rains came.

Instead of going straight to the park headquarters barracks, he went to Julianne's place. No lights were on inside the pleasant cottage, but her car was there.

He parked and walked around to the back patio. She wasn't there, either.

"Hey?" he called.

No answer.

A flash of lightning blinded him and was immediately followed by a crack of thunder so loud he instinctively ducked his head.

"Julianne," he shouted, angry for no reason except that she didn't answer, and that worried him.

A caw from the arroyo drew his attention. About a quarter mile away, he saw a lone figure jogging toward the house. Running to the truck, he grabbed an old, beat-up umbrella and raced back to the path.

Water was already running in a steady stream along the bottom of the wash. That indicated somewhere upstream of them it was pouring rain. He knew it was only a matter of minutes before it would be doing the same here. He put his head down against the wind and ran to meet her.

"Tony," Julianne said in surprise, glancing up when a running shadow was almost on her. The sky was solid cloud cover, and the late afternoon was as dark as deep twilight. "What are you doing here?"

"Come on. The storm will break any moment."

"I know. That's why I'm running."

"Here comes the rain." He opened the umbrella, which had a couple of bent spokes, and held it over her head.

When he wrapped an arm around her shoulders, she snuggled in close to him. The air had turned cold with no warning, and she wore only a thin windbreaker.

The slanting sheets of water hit the umbrella and the backs of their legs in a fury. Tony matched his stride to hers and they ran all out the last three hundred yards.

Julianne was breathless by the time they reached the patio and the slight shelter offered by the arbor. She quickly unlocked the back door.

"Get inside," he ordered. He lowered the umbrella and tossed it on the flagstones, then followed her.

He slammed the door just as hail mingled with the rain and beat against the heavy wooden portal like mean spirits demanding entrance.

"Wow, I didn't expect the storm to come up that fast or that furious." She handed Tony a paper towel and used one on her face and arms.

She laughed softly, her blood still running high with the excitement of the storm and his appearance when she hadn't expected it at all.

"Besides rescuing me, what brings you here?" she asked when their breaths stilled and only the howl of the wind and the beat of the hail filled the silence.

He leaned against the counter and crossed his long, lean legs. She remembered how they'd felt entangled with hers, so strong and powerful.

The heat was instantaneous and filled her face. She turned away in embarrassment in case he could read her wayward thoughts.

Which were never far from her mind nowadays.

"I talked to Bruce Jones and Dick Worth today," he began. "Jones wants to end the dig."

"Have you found all the important stuff?"

"No, not really. What do you know of Bruce Jones?"

The question took her by surprise. In the very dim light coming in the kitchen windows, she observed Tony's expression. He was serious, but that was all she could tell.

"Well, I knew him in Albuquerque. He taught at the community college at the same time my dad was there. My younger brother took a class under him, and he came to our house several times after my family spent a summer at a dig that he was on, too. He was our section chief."

The rain slashed the house in a constant rat-a-tat-tat. Thunder boomed over their heads and bounced off the rock formations along the arroyo.

"Why do you ask?" she finally inquired. "Do you suspect him of stealing from the Chaco site?"

Tony shook his head. "I was curious. You two seemed to go back a long way. I wondered if there was something—"

He stopped abruptly, looking chagrined, as if he'd given too much away. She realized he was...could he be...jealous?

"Bruce is old enough to be my father," she said in a chiding tone, but unable to suppress a grin.

"Not really," Tony said.

"Nearly." She sobered when he frowned at her. "I'm not and never have been interested in him."

Her guest maintained his stiff posture for another few seconds, then he exhaled a troubled sigh. "I'm going insane," he muttered.

"Join the crowd," she invited sardonically.

His handsome face remained serious and unreadable as he stared at her. After a bit, she became uncomfortable. "Do I have a smudge on my nose or something?" she finally asked.

"Or something," he agreed softly.

"Tony," she began, then couldn't think of anything to add to that.

"I think there's more to be discovered at the dig," he said, looking resolute as he changed the conversation back to business.

The hail abated, leaving sudden and total silence behind. Lightning lit up the room to noontime brilliance. The lights went out as thunder engulfed the small house.

"I have some candles," Julianne said, recovering from an instinctive wince.

"That's okay. We don't need them. Unless it makes you feel better."

"I feel fine," she said defensively. "I'm not scared of storms."

"Only of people," he murmured, but he smiled.

Her heart thudded like a bongo drum. "No, not really."

He studied her intensely again. "The other night, Wednesday night, you were trembling when things got pretty hot between us. Were you afraid? Tell me the truth," he demanded softly, insistently.

"No. Maybe a little," she added at his keen gaze. "But the times we've kissed, you didn't push me further than I wanted to go, Tony. You never have. I don't think you ever would."

"God, Julianne, don't say things like that." He shoved a hand through his hair, frustration showing on his face as another flash of lightning lit the room.

She felt as if the bolt hit her heart. From her parents' happy marriage, she'd thought when she fell in love that the object of her affections would love her, too. She'd thought that was the way nature arranged things. But all she'd discovered about falling in love was the uncertainty of it.

"Why? It's the truth. That's what you asked for."

He stared out the window, seemingly deep in thoughts as gloomy as the storm outside.

"What's bothering you?" she asked.

"That you'll expect more from me than I can give," he told her, his gaze level and honest.

She digested the words and their meaning, felt them drop into the deep, vast abyss where something innocent and full of hope had fallen a long time ago.

Swallowing hard, she dredged up a smile. "Well, it's just my luck. Meet the man of my dreams and he's commitmentphobic." She sighed dramatically.

He frowned, but then smiled at her in a patient, kind manner. "I didn't mean to sound like an egotistical SOB. I just don't want to hurt you."

"I think that's the nicest thing anyone ever said to me," she said sincerely. "However, I'm a big girl, Tony. I take responsibility for my own welfare, including that of my heart." She finished on a brisk note and turned from him, knowing it was time to change the subject before she burst into tears and/or dived into his comforting embrace. That would be just too humiliating.

His eyes followed her when she went to the fridge and peered inside. It was really quite dark by now, and she couldn't see. She lit two fat, lilac-scented candles and placed one on the table and one on the counter.

"Let's see, I have cheese, eggs and bacon. The stove is gas, so we can cook. Shall we eat?"

"I should go," he began, then simply looked at her.

Ignoring him and the clamor in her blood, she got out the food, lit a burner with a match and put the bacon in a skillet. "I hate to eat alone."

"Then I'll stay." He rose and came to her, kissing her once before letting her go. After the simple but satisfying meal, during which they mostly gazed into each other's eyes, he insisted on helping with the cleanup duties. When they were done, she turned to him.

"Jules," he said, then paused, as if he were marshaling his arguments on why he shouldn't be there, why he should leave, why they shouldn't give in to madness…

She lifted her arms and laid her palms against his chest. His heart sped up. "Feel my heart," she invited, pressing her hands harder against him.

"Jules," he murmured again, closing his eyes.

When he looked at her again, there were no more question in those dark, intriguing depths. He swung her up into his arms. "Where?"

She pointed down the hall. A flash of lightning sizzled over the cottage. He paused while their eyes adjusted to the dimness again, then he walked steadily along the short hall and paused at the first door.

"Yes," she told him.

He carried her into the bedroom and set her on her feet beside the bed. Catching her face between his big, careful hands, he kissed her again and again, each kiss going deeper than any she'd ever shared with another.

Tony felt a tremor go through Julianne, but he sensed no fear in her. Instead she gave a little cry of demand when he lifted his head. He smiled at her as his hands went to their clothing.

When at last she stood before him like a slender, perfect Venus, he took in everything about her in a glance before taking her into his arms again.

She was satin and velvet, and just touching her

drove him higher, faster, further than anyone ever had in his life. He groaned when she licked his neck and breathed her quick breaths against his throat, destroying any logical thoughts he might have possessed.

"Nothing matters," he whispered fiercely. "Nothing but you and this moment. What you do to me shouldn't be legal." He managed a chuckle and felt her answering laughter.

"It probably isn't," she said. "But I don't care."

Her low declaration excited him as much as her sweet touches over his torso. She sounded happy, excited, pleased.

All the things he felt.

When she tipped her head against his arm, he kissed her again. It was like flying, like breathing dragon fire and living to tell of it. Except he never would. Being with her like this was their secret, theirs alone....

Julianne loved the feel of his skin on hers, the crash of his heart as the excitement built to unbearable heights. She reveled in the feel of his lips, the softness, the firmness, the way he moved over her mouth, then the brush of his tongue, the slide into her mouth and the playful meeting with her tongue.

She'd been kissed, but never like this. "Can't breathe," she managed to gasp at one point. "Can't think."

He explored the lobe of her ear. "Do you really need to...or want to?"

She shook her head. He laughed and she loved the sound of it. "Tony…" She wasn't sure what she wanted to say.

"Shh," he said.

He swept the covers out of the way, guided her onto the bed and lay on his side, his head supported by his hand.

Tony gazed at her as if entranced. He wanted to tell her things—like how beautiful he thought she was and how exciting it was just to look at her and how he wanted to go slow, so she would know for sure she could trust him.

But she wasn't having any of that. "Tony," she said. It was a demand. She pulled his face to hers. He let her take the kiss, then waited patiently while she explored his body. He couldn't keep the smile from his face as she gave him quick glances, as if to see whether he was enjoying what she did.

Minutes or hours later he took them a step further. He moved his leg so his thigh rested over both hers, watching to make sure she didn't feel trapped by his greater weight.

Julianne was lost to the world as he gently searched the hollows of her throat, then down the center of her body until he finally touched one engorged nipple. She panted as he sucked at the tender spot. When he raised his head, she uttered a low moan of protest.

"You make me burn. You make me…want."

"You don't know what wanting is," he said. "You don't know the half of it."

"Show me." She ran her hands over his chest, down his sides, onto his hips. She kissed across his chest and lingered at each nipple. "Show me," she challenged.

Tony stared into her eyes and was both humbled and excited by what he saw. Hunger. Challenge. A readiness to go wherever he led. "Julianne," he said, but couldn't think of another word to add.

"Show me," she murmured, leaning into him, pressing those hard-tipped breasts against him until he couldn't think straight.

He caressed her slender body until he knew every line and indentation from her head to her waist. After that, he stroked down the smooth skin of her abdomen.

When she made a slight sound, he bent to her trembling mouth and claimed her again and again. When he felt the hunger build in her, he stroked downward, combing his fingers through the soft curls at the Venus mound.

When the need became too great, he explored the treasure beyond that. She moved her legs apart.

The sweet, unconscious invitation melted the last barrier from his mind. He delved into the hot honey of her.

"Ohh," she crooned, pressing upward, her hands grasping his shoulders as the flames rose between them. "Tony," she said, urgent, demanding.

He heard the plea, the strained note of passion. "I've dreamed of this all week."

"Yes. Oh, yes."

She was liquid fire and passionate demand, innocent impatience and instinctive knowledge. He shook with the effort at control as he caressed her completely.

She did the same to him, exploring him with a gentleness that wasn't necessary, but he didn't ask for harder, faster. That would come later, after he'd let her satisfy her curiosity—and after he'd satisfied the hunger that shook through her each time he stroked the tender bud of her desire.

He moved away while he took care of protection. When he stroked her most secret places once more, Julianne gave herself over to him, clinging desperately as the world went crazy. Tony grasped at control when he felt her pulse against his hand. "Now," he said.

He was gentle but thorough as he claimed the prize that had taunted him, staying just beyond his reach in each dream he'd had of them since that first hectic encounter.

Once they were fully merged, he let her rest before he began the sweet, mind-boggling task of building her hunger once more. "I can't believe this," she said a few minutes later as she stirred restlessly in his arms.

"I can." He laughed and kissed her until they were both breathless. "We're good together."

"Yes," she agreed with no false modesty. "More," she said, nipping at his ear, then laughing playfully as she teased him. "I want more."

He was willing to give her the moon, the stars and everything in between.

Chapter Ten

Tony woke Sunday to an overcast sky and a warm body snuggled against his.

Julianne.

A shaft of something so painful and exciting and wondrous went through him at such a furious pace, he didn't have time to figure out what it was.

With just the tips of his fingers, he explored the smooth skin from her shoulder to her thigh. His body reacted predictably.

For the first time since he could remember, he didn't want to get up. He wasn't one to malinger in the sack, but this bed belonged to Julianne and he didn't want to leave it. Okay, he didn't want to leave her, he admitted.

"Awake already?" she asked. "It's only seven."

"That's late for me."

"On Sunday, too?"

"Yep."

He leaned over to kiss her neck.

"Is it raining?"

"Look out the window," he suggested.

"I can't. My eyes won't open yet."

"It's overcast. Probably more rain on the way."

"A great day to stay in bed," she murmured, eyes still closed, but a smile touching the corners of her mouth.

He kissed her there. "I'll fix breakfast. Do you want cereal or would you prefer cereal?"

She laughed and turned over so she could face him. "Hot oatmeal is good on a cold morning. Or bacon and eggs. How about pancakes? Yummy."

With any other woman, he'd have found this exchange mindless, but with her…it was fun, a sort of prelude to other things.

His breath caught in his throat. "Maybe I'm not as hungry as I thought," he murmured, kissing along her jaw.

"Oh, I think you are," she said in a deliciously sexy voice, moving her thigh between his.

The morning began as the night had ended, with them so deep into passion the world could have blown apart and neither would have noticed. He couldn't get enough of kissing and touching, breathing in her essence, hearing the little gasps and cries she made. He loved the way she said his name as she came apart.

Later, alone in the shower while she whipped up the pancakes, he worried about their involvement. It made no sense to get carried away, and he wouldn't. All he had to do was keep it light and enjoyable. When his job was finished here, he would move on, their time together a pleasant memory for both of them.

For some reason all his arguments with his conscience or whatever part was bothering him seemed futile. He would miss her when he left, and that was a fact.

Ten minutes later, dried and dressed once more, he entered the warm kitchen that smelled of pancakes, bacon and other good things. His heart gave a gigantic leap. He helped himself to coffee, then turned the bacon while she carefully placed blueberries in an even pattern on the pancakes.

"I like a blueberry in each bite, don't you?" she asked, giving him a playful glance.

He smiled and shrugged while every muscle in his body quietly contorted itself into a knot. After setting the table and pouring coffee, he joined her when she brought their plates over and took her place.

Sitting across from her, he felt another odd sensation. He wasn't sure what it was, but—and this was really strange—it felt safe to sit here like this, just the two of them, in this quiet place, safe and secure, unlike times in the past when life had been turmoil and pain.

"You look so serious," she said.

"I was remembering things."

"Such as?"

"When my sister, Krista, and I were kids." The memory came back to him with the gloomy texture of the clouds that had preceded the storm yesterday. "When we first met our foster parents, we were excited and a little scared. I didn't let anyone see that, of course."

She nodded.

"The house was the nicest we'd ever lived in and in the nicest neighborhood. We each had our own room. It seemed too good to be true. And it was." He inhaled slowly, released the breath in a rush.

"What a terrible thing to go through. Adults are supposed to protect children, yet so often we don't. When he beat Krista, that's when you went to your cousin and the three of you ran away?"

He nodded.

Tears filled the stormy gray eyes across from him, ran down her cheeks. "Tony—"

"Don't," he said. "I'm not asking for pity."

"I know."

He wasn't sure what he was trying to say. He

breathed deeply again. "Last night was great," he told her, "but all good things come to an end."

She nodded, a hint of sadness in her eyes. "Don't worry, Tony. I'm not going to demand more from you. Let's take things one day at a time. Okay?"

Her smile was so sweet it melted the knotty muscles inside him. Her eyes held an impish quality. He had to smile. "Yeah."

They stayed together all day, reading the paper, catching a football game, napping, making love, laughing, making love.

It wasn't until he was leaving that he noticed the two pieces of pottery on top of the armoire she used as a china cabinet.

Julianne couldn't believe she'd spent the morning at the police station, filling out a report on how she'd gotten the priceless artifact and coming under suspicion all over again for being a thief. It was getting tiresome.

There were two pots—one was a corrugated design from a very early period of Chaco culture. The other was a large, black-glazed piece. They were gifts from Josiah out of gratitude for her help at the birth of his son. The first pot was valuable and had been confiscated. The larger piece was now in her car.

Had she seen distrust in Tony's eyes for a second as she'd explained? His expression had shut down as tight as a professional gambler's, disclosing nothing of his thoughts or feelings.

He hadn't clarified them to her when she'd left the station after having given her statement and signing the typed copy. Neither had he mentioned seeing her later today.

In fact, he'd shifted to the role of the steely-eyed investigator once again.

She wanted to smash something, such as the blasted pot in the trunk of her car. Other than that, she wished she hadn't signed a two-year contract to run the clinic. She had over a year to go and she would rather not see Special Investigator Anthony Aquilon ever again.

The idea hurt so badly she winced.

Maybe Tony would get transferred to another park. But that grim possibility wouldn't happen until the thefts at Chaco Canyon were resolved. She sighed heavily and put the troubling introspection aside.

Going in the side door of the clinic, she used the quiet morning hours to clear out the eternal paperwork.

Edmund had finished the audit last week, but she hadn't seen the report yet. With her luck, he would probably find some part of her record keeping totally wrong and she would be accused of embezzling or something equally stupid.

So, just lock her up and throw away the key. She

smacked the heel of her hand down on the desk for emphasis, but only succeeded in hurting herself.

Rubbing her hand, she tried to smile, to think positive thoughts, to pretend she hadn't seen that possible flash of suspicion in Tony's dark, fathoms-deep eyes.

At eleven, a knock on the front door interrupted her concentration. While the clinic wasn't open on Mondays, and the extra time was voluntary on her part, she did see a few patients if necessary.

Spotting a very pregnant young girl at the entrance, Julianne opened the main door. "Are you alone?" she asked, peering over the woman's shoulder toward the parking area. Other than her vehicle, no other was visible.

The girl didn't answer, but bent forward and pressed her hands against her thighs as a contraction tightened across her body. Julianne timed it.

When the mother-to-be could move again, Julianne led her to a birthing room. "Have you been here before?" she asked, getting out a gown and disposable pads.

The patient shook her head.

Julianne thought she looked sixteen, seventeen at the most. Pity filled her. This was a young girl, alone and frightened, just as she'd been at ten, coming home and finding her mother's body.

"I'm Julianne Martin. I'm the midwife here at the clinic. Change into this gown, and we'll get you in bed so you'll be more comfortable. Have you seen a doctor?"

The young woman shook her head.

"Is this your first baby?"

A nod.

"Is there someone you would like me to call?" Julianne asked.

Again the patient gave a despairing shake of the head.

Julianne kept up a stream of light chatter, telling the frightened mother what to expect and when. She also called one of the R.N.s to come in and help. She was relieved to find her oldest and most experienced nurse at home. A first baby and no medical care meant they hadn't a clue to the mother's or child's health needs.

While doing the necessary prep, then the forms, which she filled out as the teenager rested between several more contractions, Julianne wondered what she would do if she were in this situation.

This nearly silent girl, who said she was eighteen, insisted she had no next of kin.

After careful questioning, Julianne learned her patient was from California and had been on a bus. She was heading for her grandmother's house in a town near Albuquerque. When she'd realized the baby was coming three weeks early, she'd gotten off in town and looked in the phone book for someplace to go. That's how she'd found the clinic.

Finally she let Julianne see her driver's license. Erin was her name, and she was eighteen.

"Would you like me to call your grandmother?"

"Not yet. I will. Later. I promise."

When the nurse arrived, Julianne and Erin were both panting hard. "Big push," Julianne said. "Grab your knees, hold your breath and push!"

A few minutes later she laid a lovely little girl in the mother's arms. The baby howled indignantly.

The three women laughed.

"I love her," Erin said, cuddling the child against her neck. "She's beautiful. I love her."

"She is beautiful," Julianne agreed. "Babies are the most wonderful things. They trust us completely to care for them and help them grow up and teach them to be adults."

Erin's dark eyes filled with tears. "It's a big responsibility."

"Won't the father help?" Julianne asked as gently as possible.

"No."

This was said with such flat certainty that Julianne wanted to put her head down and cry, too.

"But my grammy will," Erin added.

Julianne smoothed the fluffy hair on the baby's head. "That's good," she said. "It's good to have someone." She knew, whatever the crises in her own life, she wouldn't face them alone. Her dad and brothers would stand by her, no matter what.

And so would Tony. She knew no child of his would ever be abandoned.

* * *

Julianne let Erin and Kyla, named after the grandmother, stay at the clinic to rest for a few days before the two resumed the trip. She worried about a baby that tiny being on a bus where someone might have a serious illness of some kind.

She slept in her office, partly because she felt responsible for the security of the clinic and partly because she didn't want Erin to feel alone, not with a new baby to care for.

"I wonder if the bus driver will let me back on the bus since I only have the ticket stub?" Erin looked at Julianne with an anxious expression.

Julianne figured the girl was worried about money. An idea came to her. "My family lives in Albuquerque," she said. "I haven't visited them since the Fourth of July. If you like, you can ride up with me tomorrow."

Erin's dark eyes glowed. "Really?"

"Yes. The clinic is closed on Fridays, so the timing is perfect. I'll call my father tonight to let him know."

They planned the details of the trip. Julianne was pleased that doing so seemed to restore a bounce to Erin's spirits. The cheerfulness was good for the baby, too.

That evening, once the clinic was finally cleaned— Erin insisted on helping them clean up—Julianne went home, called her father, got an enthusiastic okay to her visit, then packed enough clothing for the weekend.

Before leaving the cottage, she stared at the telephone, unable to decide whether she should call Tony or not, to inform him of her plans.

She didn't owe him an explanation, she concluded. It wasn't as if she were under house arrest or anything like that. Besides, he hadn't bothered to leave any messages for her all week. So she could leave with a clear conscience.

However, she did call Chief Windover's office and tell his secretary that she'd be gone for the weekend. Next she called Diana to cancel their Friday luncheon.

"Have a pleasant trip," Diana told her. "I, uh, have something to ask you, something personal."

Julianne assumed it was about Tony. "Ask away," she invited as if she hadn't a care in the world.

"Edmund has asked me to go to a special movie on the ancient cultures at the Chaco Museum tomorrow night."

"That sounds like fun," Julianne said when the silence grew lengthy between them.

"Then you don't mind?"

Julianne drew a blank for a second, then she realized Diana thought *she* might have a prior claim on the man. "I don't mind at all. I'm so glad you two hit it off."

"We ran into each other at the grocery last Sunday

and got to talking. We, uh, went out to dinner. He's so much fun, isn't he?"

Julianne wondered if they were talking about the same man. "And smart, too," she added with a laugh, not committing herself on the "fun" part.

Diana joined in the laughter. "Feel perfectly free to pursue our other mutual hunk. I think Tony has a thing for you," she added in a teasing note.

"He thinks I'm a pot thief," Julianne said with a wry twist to the words.

"Well, men are slow on the uptake."

At ease with each other again, they said farewell and hung up. Julianne huffed out an exasperated breath. She wasn't going to speak to the detective again and she wasn't going to think about last Sunday and what they had been doing while Diana and Edmund were discovering each other.

After attending physical therapy classes with her father on Saturday morning, then jogging with him that afternoon, they had a cookout that evening with her two brothers. It was wonderful being in the bosom of her loving, albeit teasing, family for the weekend.

"So," her older brother, Calhoon, inquired, "who is this new man in your life?"

Julianne had to swallow hard before answering. "He's not new. Special Investigator Aquilon is hot on the trail of the thieves again. Unfortunately the trail led straight to my house." She explained about the pots.

"That young man needs a lesson in gratitude, not to mention involving others in his crimes," her father said, referring to Josiah.

"True." Cal peaked his fingers together while he considered. "Still, Aquilon didn't arrest you again, so he must think you're innocent."

Julianne felt herself grow warmer at the term. She felt she knew much more about life and innocence and trusting others than she had three weeks go. That was the day she'd tried to do a good deed, had met Tony and gotten accused of grand theft. Life had been a roller-coaster ride ever since, and all of it on the downhill side.

Well, not quite all.

"He'd better know she's innocent," Sam, two years her junior, stated.

Her younger brother was the more physically aggressive of the two boys. He'd loved sports growing up, but now ironically he was a computer geek who was paid to find flaws and develop firewalls in operating systems so the government could repel hackers. He'd helped her set up the bookkeeping system at the clinic by phone.

"It'll come out okay," her father assured her after they'd discussed the case thoroughly and she'd extolled the wonders of Chaco Canyon and its secrets.

Later, after her brothers left, she and her dad

lingered in the comfortable sunroom that had become their family room. "I've worried about you," he murmured.

She glanced at him in surprise. "I'm fine. I love my job. The location is beautiful, my cottage is a sweet place, and I really don't think I'm in danger of going to jail." Her smile was meant to reassure him.

"But you haven't really been dating. Or thought about marriage."

"Neither have the boys."

He waved that aside, as if to indicate he wasn't worried about them. "They didn't come home and find their mother lying in a pool of blood. In spite of growing up in a household of men, you're wary of the opposite sex. I noticed that, while you were in high school and college. I worry you'll never get over the trauma of that day."

The horror of it came back to her—the blood, her mother's lifeless body, the incomprehension in her ten-year-old mind during those first few minutes.

"Mom? Mom, wake up. Wake up!"

But even then, she'd realized her mother was never going to see her again, no matter that her eyes were wide open and staring.

A shudder went through her. "Did you get over it?" she asked.

He sighed and took her hand. "She was the love of my life," he said simply. "So are you and the boys, each in your own special way."

She squeezed and released his bony, capable fingers and went to the window to stare out at the stars, which seemed so far away and indifferent to human desires, not at all the way they were that night at the cottage when she'd trusted Tony completely.

"I've accepted the things that can't be changed," she said slowly. "I've grieved, as an adult, for Mother. She'll never meet my husband, should I ever have one. She'll never know my children. I think I resent that most of all—that she never got a chance to be the loving grandmother I know she would be." She turned back to her father, smiling in spite of the sadness in her heart. "But I still have you and Cal and Sam. My children will, too. And that's something."

Her father came to her, locking her in his protective embrace as he had when she was a child, making everything all better for those few, precious moments.

Sunday morning, Julianne kissed her dad good-bye and headed west once more, refreshed in mind, body and spirit.

Erin and little Kyla were safely sheltered with their grandmother, who'd been delighted to have them. The girl had called her parents and told them where she was and that she planned on staying there.

Julianne was sure Grammy Kyla would help the young mother sort her life out.

Turning up the radio, she listened to a female vocalist sing about the pain of first love and its loss, and thought of her relationship, or lack thereof, with Tony. He was the first man outside of her family that she'd let herself trust completely.

Although he'd warned her that his heart wasn't involved and there was no "happily ever after" in store for them, in the hidden, hopeful places of her own heart, she'd thought there was. Silly heart.

"I know I'll love again," she sang softly with the radio. Her throat closed and remained that way for a painful minute. She managed a rueful smile. Of course she would love again. Life wasn't over at twenty-six.

An hour before she arrived in Gallup, she pulled into a service station and filled the gas tank. Going inside the market, she selected a soda and peanut butter crackers for lunch, paid and headed out again.

She was so deep in her own thoughts she nearly missed spotting the man who drove past her in a blue pickup.

"Josiah," she muttered, staring after the truck as it left the station and got back on the interstate. "Hey," she called after it.

Before he could get completely out of sight, she was in her car and on his trail.

Once on the highway with the pickup in sight, she slowed and followed at a careful distance behind the truck. Luckily, its bright hue was easy to track among the other vehicles on the highway. When he turned off on a state road, so did the SUV behind him. Julianne was able to hide behind it as the three of them sped along the road.

When Josiah turned right into a state campground with plenty of trees for cover, she passed by, then turned around a quarter of a mile down the road and returned, entering the shady camping area cautiously. She spotted the truck at once and turned into an empty camping spot on a winding road opposite the one where Josiah and his family were.

She fished her cell phone out of her purse and punched in Tony's cell number, which he'd given her in case she came up with any information on the case.

"Hello?" a familiar masculine voice barked into her ear.

Her heart clenched up. She ignored it. "This is Julianne. I found Josiah," she said.

There was an instant of silence, then, "Go on," he said.

She told Tony where the couple were located. He told her to go home. "I'm staying until I get some answers about that pottery," she informed him.

"I'll be right there. Stay out of sight. Don't do anything stupid," he ordered.

After hanging up, she ducked down in the seat and peered through the cottonwoods toward the other camp.

"I already have. I fell in love with you," she muttered as if her nemesis were in the car with her. "And that *was* stupid."

Chapter Eleven

Worry eating a hole in his stomach, Tony ignored the speed limit and tore along the interstate highway to the campground Julianne had mentioned. He prayed that Josiah and his partners-in-crime wouldn't spot her.

What would they do?

He couldn't think further ahead than getting Josiah under observation and Julianne safe. Forty minutes after he started, he slowed and turned onto the state road. A few minutes after that, he arrived at his destination.

The setup was as Julianne had described. The blue pickup and the small trailer were parked in a camping spot. There was a tablecloth and cooler on the picnic table. A woman sat in an aluminum-framed chair and rocked a baby.

He kept his baseball cap pulled low over his eyes, although the couple had never seen him face-to-face, as he drove past the site and around the circle to the entrance again, then onto the side track where he'd noticed Julianne's car hidden in a thicket of cotton-woods. He pulled in behind her and got out, his pulse leaping as she smiled at him from her front seat.

"Do you know where Josiah is?" he asked, leaning his forearms on her car door and giving her a once-over.

She wore pink shorts and a white knit top with pink trim. Her hair was pulled into a pink scrunchy, making her look around sixteen, instead of the twenty-six he knew she was. He remembered how smooth and shapely her legs had felt meshed with his and quickly shut off that memory.

"He's in the trailer. His wife came outside a few minutes ago with their baby, but I haven't seen him since he arrived and went inside."

"You're positive he's still there?"

"Yes." A worried frown knit two tiny lines over her nose. "Are you going to confront him?"

Before answering, Tony studied the campsite through the thick screen of cottonwood branches. The door of the mobile home was visible, so it was unlikely Josiah could have sneaked out.

He suppressed an urge to go over there, burst into the place like a TV cop and choke the truth out of the man. "I think we would be better off putting him under surveillance."

"Do you think he's still working with someone at the Chaco dig?"

"He could be. We know he gave pots to you at two different times, so he had access over a period of weeks."

He paused as the mother laid the sleeping baby in her lap, lowered the chair back a couple of notches and obviously prepared to take a nap herself. Through the dappled shade, a streak of sunlight haloed the young mother's head, giving her an aura of innocence, like a Madonna of the woods.

Tony thought of Julianne and her enthusiasm for babies. Diana had told him of the trip to Albuquerque, which was spurred by Julianne's concern for the girl who'd stopped by the clinic to have her child.

If nothing else had convinced him of her innocence in the thievery, this would have. The good deed was so like the nurse-midwife, always getting right in the middle of her patients' problems and helping out if she could.

A man could love a woman like that.

He heard her sigh softly. "It was so difficult to sit here rather than face Josiah and demand the truth," she said in a low voice that carried an undertone of discouragement.

He wanted to take her into his arms and comfort her for placing her trust in someone who didn't deserve it. He swallowed hard and beat the mushy feeling into submission.

"You can go home now," he told her, speaking harsher than he'd meant to. "I'll take it from here."

Her frown deepened. "You can't watch them all the time. Do you have someone to help you?"

"Sure, Chuck is working with me."

She opened her mouth, then closed it.

He prepared for an argument and realized he looked forward to it. Fighting with her was more fun than anything he could think of to do with another person. He gave an internal groan. He had to stop thinking like that!

"Okay," she said, surprising the heck out of him. "I'll take off. Call me if you need anything."

"Right."

He moved his vehicle so she could back out. Spotting a better position to observe the couple without being noticed, he parked at another camping site and prepared for a long afternoon and night. Good thing he'd brought water and some food to get him through.

This time, there would be no soft feminine body to curl around to keep each other warm. He'd missed that this past week as he'd doggedly rejected the need to see her, to say hello, to bask in the honey of her smile....

* * *

Wednesday Julianne sat at her favorite place under the arbor over the patio. Nights were growing shorter, and dusk had already fallen by the time she'd had tomato soup and a grilled cheese sandwich for dinner. She munched on an apple as her dessert.

The slam of a car door alerted her that someone had stopped out front. She reluctantly peered around the edge of the cottage so she could see the carport and driveway.

"Bruce," she called, more than a bit surprised. "Hi, I'm out here."

He waved and came around the side of the house to join her in the pleasant shadows.

"Iced tea?" she asked. "Or a soda?"

"The tea would be great. I'm parched from the digging today. It's slow going at the depth we're at."

"Are you finding a lot of artifacts?" she asked, speaking through the open kitchen window as she prepared his glass of tea. She returned to the patio.

"Not now. The deeper we go, the older the culture and the scarcer the finds."

"It must be exciting to discover a pot or basket, though, and know someone made it nearly a thousand years ago, that there were people here then, carrying on their crafts, having families, making lives for themselves."

His smile was weary. "The wonder wanes after the first ten or so years."

She nodded in understanding. "But you've made important finds. That has to be satisfying."

"Yes."

He stared at the landscape and sipped the tea without speaking for several minutes. Used to her father and brothers, she allowed him the time and space he needed.

"How are things going at the clinic?" he asked after a bit, his tone gentler than before.

"Good, I think. Edmund didn't indicate any problems with the bookkeeping, so that's a relief."

"I understand another pot was found here at your house." He shot her a questioning look.

Her spirits took a dip for the worse. "Yes. Josiah gave me two. Unfortunately, one of them was a priceless artifact. Tony said it was a corrugated design that was very valuable. It had little elongated dots all over the surface of the pot."

A look of anger came over her guest's face. As curator of the ancient-culture museum, the thefts would naturally make him furious with the transgressors.

"I'm sure Josiah wasn't thinking about the loss to the cultural history," she murmured in his defense. "With a wife and baby and the loss of his job, I'm sure he was only thinking of the money he needed in order to make it until he could find work again."

"Yeah," Bruce said without a softening in his manner.

The urge to tell him that she'd found the couple

was almost impossible to ignore. The fact that Bruce was a family friend made it that much harder. She knew she could trust him with the information, but he looked so angry she was afraid he would go to the campground and demand that Josiah tell him who else was in on the plot.

Which was exactly how she felt.

"The other pot Josiah gave you wasn't an important one, I understand," Bruce continued.

"Right. I think he made it. I watched him and his wife each 'throw' a pot, as they called it, one day when I went out to check on her."

"Tony hasn't come across any clues?"

She shook her head. "Not since the last time I spoke with him." That much was true.

Bruce finished the tea and rose. "I've got to get home, shower and change for a night class I'm teaching this semester. It's a three-hour course and everyone falls asleep the last hour." He chuckled suddenly. "It could be worse. It could be three nights a week instead of only one."

She laughed with him as they walked to his vehicle through the quiet twilight. The hum of an engine surprised her. Glancing toward the road, she saw Tony stop at the curb. He motioned for Bruce to come out before he drove in.

"See you," the archeology expert said. He waved to Tony, then backed out of the short drive and left.

Tony pulled into the space behind her car.

"Anyone else here that I should know about?" he asked as he came around the SUV.

"No. Are you going to be grumpy all evening?" She kept her tone level with an effort.

He stopped in front of her. "Maybe."

After five awkward seconds, she gave in and invited him to join her on the patio. He nodded. When she offered iced tea, he accepted.

Going back outside, tea in hand, she placed the glasses on the side table between their two chairs and settled into her usual place.

"Thanks," he said, accepting the glass, then taking a long drink as if he'd been tracking through the desert for several hours.

"How are things going with Josiah?" she finally asked when the silence grew unbearable.

"Well, he's not making any sudden moves. He and his wife are acting as camp hosts. They don't have to pay any fees that way. He's picking up odd jobs at the gas stations on the interstate."

"That's good. It's so hard to find steady work in this area. With the mine shutting down a couple of months ago, it's even more difficult. How does a community convince companies to locate here?"

After a minute of silence, Tony shrugged. "I don't know. Isn't that why we elect politicians?" he asked cynically. "Aren't they supposed to address society's problems?"

She didn't answer.

He let out a deep breath. "Sorry. I'm not good company tonight. I shouldn't have stopped."

His dark eyes were black pits of frustration when he glanced at her.

"Seriously, how are things going with the case? Is anyone watching Josiah tonight?"

"Yeah." He swallowed a chip with a generous dollop of salsa. "Chuck is supervising the watch detail. He's got some men doing drive-by checks on every patrol. I don't think Josiah is going to head for parts unknown soon. He did drive out to see his mother yesterday. Did she call you?"

Julianne shook her head. "Why would she?" she demanded. "She knows I would have to tell the authorities. Her son would be arrested, maybe sent to jail."

Tony caught her wrist as she waved her hand expressively. "That big heart is going to get you into trouble one of these days."

Pulling away, she frowned at him, irritated by the conversation, by the fact that he was here now when he hadn't stopped all last week and by the stirrings inside her that urged her to throw herself in his arms and demand that he kiss her until they collapsed in a passionate tangle.

She clenched her hands in her lap and sat perfectly still until she got over those ridiculous notions.

"Why did you stop?" she asked in a subdued voice.

"I saw Bruce's pickup. What did he want?"

"I don't know. He asked about the case, of course,

but like you, he seems discouraged about solving it. I guess I didn't know it would be so difficult."

"I'm beginning to think we're looking in the wrong place."

"What do you mean?"

"Josiah may have had a one-time shot at getting some of the pieces—"

"He gave me pots at two different times."

"Okay," Tony acceded, "a two-time shot, but he doesn't seem to have any connections to a cluster of thefts that have taken place in the pueblos over the past year. The problem is that no one we've watched seems to be in on it. Maybe we're chasing a mirage. Maybe there's no ring and therefore no ringleader."

"What about that guy, Lovelace? The announcement of his arrest was on the local news. Maybe he's the ringleader."

"He admitted he'd heard about the finds in a bar that night and decided rather on the spur of the moment—since he happened to be stone broke—to see what he could find. He'd also heard about you being arrested. He thought he could turn the heat on you and away from himself with that brilliant ploy about you selling him artifacts. The shards he had were too small to be of value. At any rate, we didn't have enough to hold him, so Chuck escorted him to the county line and sent him on his way."

Tony's attractive mouth thinned in disgust, and Julianne realized he'd never believed Lovelace.

"Thank you for not believing him," she said simply.

Her eyes locked with the moody ones across the small table. She wasn't sure what her gaze was telling him, but she couldn't look away. Longing grew in her until she was filled to the bursting point.

He took a long drink of tea and drained the glass, then set it down with a dull thud. "I missed you this week."

Unable to speak, she nodded.

"I had to stay away," he continued with dogged determination. "We can't just…just…"

"Give in to passion?" she suggested, sounding as breathless as he was desperate.

He clenched his large but gentle hands and nodded. "It's crazy to feel this way. I've never let myself go insane over a woman before."

"If you don't kiss me, I'm going to scream," she said softly.

He laced his fingers between his knees and stared at the flagstones at his feet. "I know the feeling. Every time I've passed here, it felt as if the steering wheel had a mind of its own. It was all I could do not to stop."

"You did tonight."

He gave her a fierce look. "Yeah. I couldn't resist—" He stopped abruptly, as if giving away too much.

She saw him swallow as if his throat was as clogged as hers before he stared at the flagstones once more. "Tony," she said on a whisper.

He muttered a curse and stood.

She rose and laid a hand on his arm. "Don't go. I don't want you to."

His gaze was haunted. "Do you think I want to? After once staying here with you, knowing all the sweetness of your lips, the feel of you in my arms, do you think it's been easy this past week?"

"Then why didn't you come by?" she demanded, her heart beating very fast.

"Because I'm on a case. Because you're involved in some way I can't figure out."

She dropped her hand as if burned by a sudden lava flow. "I'll never forgive you for that," she said in a stricken voice. "Never."

He gave her a level stare. "I know, but that's the way life works. Every good thing turns out to be a dream. Or a lie."

With that, he walked around the corner of the house. In a few seconds, she heard his truck start, then the sound of tires on the gravel driveway as he left.

The night air seemed to chill all around her. Sitting in the chair, she crossed her arms over her chest, holding on so the hurt wouldn't shred her dignity and make her scream like a banshee into the night.

A *whuff* of wings over the arroyo, followed by a squeal, signaled the catching of a small animal by a night predator.

She felt as if her own heart had been skewered,

and wondered how a person lived with the knowledge that the one she'd trusted completely thought the very worst of her.

Very carefully, she rose and took the platter and glasses inside. She washed and put away the dishes, then went to her room.

She showered and prepared for bed, aware of a bone-deep weariness that had nothing to do with working eleven hours that day and everything to do with being in love and feeling foolish and wishing she'd never met a certain special investigator.

A litany ran through her dreams that night.

I'll never forgive you.

I know.

I'll never forgive you.

I know.

The odd thing was that she couldn't tell who was saying the words.

Chapter Twelve

Tony listened intently, the familiar sound of an engine hitting on five pistons instead of six alerting him to nearby action. He remained still as the blue pickup left the campsite. Josiah was driving. His wife waved goodbye from the trailer and closed the door against the cool morning air.

After giving the young father a head start, Tony followed at a distance. To his surprise, Josiah drove to town. There he checked in at the state employment office and went to three different garages, leaving each one after being inside five or ten minutes.

Was he asking about a job?

If he'd fled the area to keep from being caught for

having stolen goods, why would he return to a place where he could possibly be spotted and apprehended?

Tony concluded the younger man felt safe now that nothing had happened during the month since he'd given Julianne the pots to deliver for him.

Letting the truck get a block ahead after leaving the third garage, Tony tailed Josiah to another part of town.

The culprit went to the clinic. To his consternation, Julianne's car was in its usual parking spot. Friday wasn't an open day at the medical facility, but like him, she used the quiet time to catch up.

His heart lurched crazily before he forced it to slow. He had to stay cool and keep his thinking clear of emotion. Seeing no sign of a weapon on the man, Tony decided to stay hidden and see what developed.

When Julianne opened the side door of the clinic—just as Tony knew she would—Josiah went inside. The door closed. Tony prayed she hadn't locked it.

Julianne glanced at Josiah several times as they walked down the silent corridor to the business office. Waving him to a chair, she returned to the executive position behind the desk.

"Well," she said, "what brings you here after…"

She checked the calendar. It had been the first day of the month that she'd blithely brought the stolen goods into town with the best of intentions. It was now the twenty-eighth. Three more days and the month would be gone.

"After all this time?" she finished.

"I need your help." He gazed at her without flinching.

"I recall the last time I helped you and Mary. It landed me in jail. Perhaps you have forgotten that, or didn't your mother mention it when you visited her?"

She marveled at the hardness in her voice. She'd never been a cynic, but now, well, she didn't have a lot of faith in her fellow human beings of late. She was suspicious of everyone and mentally questioned their motives in the simplest of requests. It wasn't a good feeling.

He looked down at his clasped hands as if ashamed. She didn't let it soften her heart.

"We have no food. Mary must eat in order to have milk for the baby."

She wanted to tell him he should have thought of that before embarking on a life of crime, but thinking of the baby and its sweet innocence caught her at her weakest point. She sighed instead of ranting. His family was the reason he'd needed money so desperately.

"Tell me how you got involved in stealing the artifacts from Chaco Canyon. Who put you up to giving me those pots to deliver? Who's your contact at the dig?"

The silence stretched between them like a rubber band. Just before it snapped, he shook his head. "I can't tell you."

"You won't tell me," she corrected. She picked up the phone. "I'm calling the police. If you can't face them and admit the truth, you'd better leave while you can."

"Wait," he said, a plea in the word. "I'm sorry about getting you involved, but I had no choice. I was too scared to deliver the stolen stuff myself. The man threatened me if I didn't—"

"What man?" she demanded, leaning forward, her heart leaping into her throat. At last she was getting somewhere.

He stared at the floor, his shoulders slumped in misery.

"What was the threat?" she asked, more gently this time.

"To hurt my family. To take away our home and send me to prison."

"He would implicate himself if he tried. You would only have to tell Tony, that is, the authorities," she quickly amended, "the person's name."

Josiah lips curled in disgust. "Right. It would be my word against his, and who would believe me against a—"

He stopped and stared at the floor again.

"I believe you," she said. "Tell me his name. I'll vouch for you. I'll get help. My brother is an attorney."

He shook his head. "It's no use. If you won't help me, I must leave before someone reports me."

She stood. Bracing herself with her hands on the

desk, she demanded, "How can you expect others to help when you won't help yourself? The investigator from the park service is a decent man. He'll know what to do."

Josiah headed for the door. "He'll send me to jail. There'll be no one to take care of my wife and baby. My mother said you would help, but I should have known better than to come here. No one helps people like us."

"Don't bother with the woe-is-me act. It won't wash." Following him down the corridor, Julianne spoke to his back. "I won't help you evade the law. If you turn state's witness and name the ringleader of whoever is stealing the artifacts, you'll be treated with leniency."

"Sure," Josiah said in a tone so devoid of hope and any belief in human kindness that Julianne felt discouraged for him. "All the cops want is someone behind bars. That someone will be me."

"Tony won't let that happen," she said on a quieter note as they stopped at the door. "He'll investigate thoroughly and get to the truth, but you have to give him a direction in which to search. Don't let yourself be used as a shield for someone else. That would be the real crime."

They stood there, the silence breaking over them like ocean waves hitting the shore. Julianne wanted to stop the young father when he reached for the dead bolt knob.

"She's right," a voice said behind her. "Turn yourself in and you'll get the chance to clear your name. If I have to arrest you, it'll be harder to convince others that you're telling the truth."

"Tony!" Julianne cried softly.

The two men stood three feet apart, Julianne in the middle, and stared each other in the eye. She waited, heart pounding, for the outcome.

"I'll tell the authorities you came to me," Tony continued after a moment, speaking to the culprit. "That will weigh in your favor."

Josiah's lips curled in a sneer of disbelief. "The D.A. will hang me out to dry."

"I'll take the case to federal court." He glanced at Julianne. "I think we can switch the jurisdiction since the canyon is public land and I was the officer involved in the arrest rather than Chuck."

"That would be best," she agreed, thinking of the district attorney and his obvious ambitions.

"I'll need details," Tony told the other man. "Right now, I have to take you in and book you. Are you going to cooperate, or am I going to have to cuff you?"

Julianne felt Josiah's stoic acceptance of his fate, also his sense of defeat, when he said, "I'll go with you."

"I'll check on Mary and the baby. Everything will work out," she assured him.

Her eyes met Tony's. His expression was unreadable, but there was no welcome or gladness in those dark depths for her. He was an officer doing his job, nothing more, nothing less. It made her feel odd, as if she meant nothing to him.

"Do I need to do anything?" she asked.

"Don't leave town." He didn't crack a smile to soften the surprising advice.

"Right," she said, taken aback. "I'll be home all weekend in case you need to arrest me again."

However, after lunch, Julianne remembered Josiah's worry about his family. She left word on Tony's cell phone that she was taking food out to the mother. Three hours later she returned to her cottage, bone-weary after the shopping, then the trip out to the campground and the attempt to shore up Mary's spirits when Julianne told her of the arrest.

"He'll go to prison," the young mother had said, tears streaming down her face.

Her grief caused the baby to cry. Julianne held both of them in her arms and cried, too.

When they were calmer, she suggested Mary move to Josiah's mother's place so she would be closer to town and have some help with the baby.

"How? I don't have the pickup," Mary had replied. "The police will keep it."

"It's at the clinic. I'll check with Tony and see what's to become of it. Meanwhile I'm sure we can find someone with a hitch who can move the trailer."

All in all, she thought, changing into jogging clothes, things were moving along. With Josiah in custody, Tony would soon have the thieves rounded up and behind bars. For turning state's witness, Josiah would be freed, and best of all her name would be cleared.

At least, that's what happened in TV shows. Was it also true in real life?

Tony stared at the young man who stared back at him without any expression whatsoever. "You're lying, Josiah. Why?" he asked.

"I'm not. I was told to give the pottery to the nurse and she would take care of it. I was to get half the money she received from the buyer."

"Where did you get the stolen goods?"

"It was left at a certain place. I picked it up."

"Where?"

"Out near Standing Rock. There's a cave in the rocks on the west side. The pots were left in the cave."

"Who left them?"

Josiah shrugged. "I don't know. It was arranged by telephone." He glared defiantly at Tony. "We were going to lose our home. I had to have the money."

Tony nodded, careful not to let the pity show. Life was tough. He could vouch for that. "So how did you and the caller hook up?"

Josiah shrugged. "He called me and said he could help us if we would help him. He knew everything about me, including the arrest when I was a kid. He told me to give the box to the nurse. I did. That's all I know."

Tony gazed into the dark brown eyes across the interrogation table. Three hours and Josiah had stuck to the same story. It always came back to Julianne.

"Okay," he said, rising and heading for the door. "I'll come back tomorrow and see if we can't get a straight story out of you. You're not helping your cause by lying." He went out and closed the door behind him.

"What did you think?" he asked Chuck.

"He's scared of somebody. The question is, who?"

"That's what I think, too." He stretched and yawned. "Man, I'm beat. I'm going home to sleep tonight. Pulling double duty for a week is enough. If someone raids the Chaco dig tonight…" He left the idea hanging in midair.

Chuck walked out with him. "Lock up our guest," he told the desk sergeant on the way out of the building, then spoke to Tony again. "If Josiah doesn't change his story, you'd better tell the nurse to get a lawyer."

Tony nodded and said goodbye. He vented his feelings with a string of curses as he drove away from the police station. Setting emotion aside, he picked up his cell phone and told her the latest news. Unless she could come up with the culprit and a plausible reason she'd gotten mixed up in the stolen artifact case, things didn't look good for her future.

If she'd used him to divert suspicion from someone else, who would that someone be?

Edmund Franks? Were the two of them playing some kind of game with him and Diana?

He didn't want to think so. No one would go as far as Julianne had with him merely as a diversion.

Right. He was the greatest lover of the decade, and she hadn't been able to resist his charms.

But the question nagged at him as the sky darkened into twilight. Was he fooling himself? Maybe she hadn't been as bowled over by him as he'd been by her. Okay, life was like that. He turned into her driveway and stopped behind her car. She wasn't going to like his news. Or the person who delivered it.

He sighed. Yeah, life was tough.

The next day Cal arrived at Julianne's cottage at four in the afternoon. He brought an overnight case. "Okay if I crash here?" he asked after they exchanged hugs.

"Of course." She followed him into the spare bedroom. She'd called him as soon as Tony had left yesterday, after imparting the news that Josiah had implicated her in the artifact thievery. She'd felt betrayed in her faith in the young man…and by her feelings for Tony. She set the useless emotions aside. "Have you seen Josiah yet?"

"Yep."

"And?" she said impatiently.

"Let me change clothes, then I'll tell all," he

promised, shooing her out and closing the door. "I could use something tall and cool to drink," he called after her.

She made a pitcher of tea, then settled on the patio. Cal joined her a couple of minutes later. "Ah, it feels good to relax."

"Tell me what's going to happen," she demanded as soon as he plopped into a chair and propped his feet on the lower rail of the rustic arbor.

"You're in the clear."

"I am?" She was astonished at this news.

"Josiah is going to turn state's witness and tell all. He and his family will be given protection."

"From whom?"

"I think I'll leave that for our fearless special investigator. He's on his way to make the arrest."

No matter how much she railed against her brother's reticence, he merely smiled and shook his head. He glanced at his watch an hour later. "Let's go to the grocery store. I'm hungry for a steak. I'll even volunteer to do the grilling."

"What a hero," she muttered, casting him an annoyed glance. "Shall I drive or do you want to?"

"You can. I like having a chauffeur."

He chuckled smugly as she tried all the tricks she knew to get information out of him. "Is it someone I know?" she asked, pulling into a parking space at the store.

"Yeah."

"You are so like a brother," she told him, standing in line after they collected their groceries. "You can pay for dinner since it was your idea."

She was acutely aware of the fact that Cal had chosen three thick New York cuts for the grill. That must mean Tony intended to be at her place in time to eat with them.

Outside the store, they ran into Diana and Edmund. "Well, hello," Julianne said.

The couple returned her greeting. She introduced Cal to them and tried to gracefully move on. This wasn't a moment for socializing as far as she was concerned. Tony might be at the house waiting for them. He was going to tell her who the ringleader was. Or else.

"Edmund and I are going to a dance at the community center. It's a fund-raiser for a new fire engine. I have two extra tickets. Would you two be interested?" Diana asked.

"Not tonight," Julianne quickly answered. "We have plans."

"Another time, then. Nice to meet you, Cal," Diana said in her gracious way.

Julianne noticed the way Edmund moved closer to Diana as her brother and her friend exchanged farewells. She realized he was letting Cal know Diana was taken.

For a second she wished Tony felt enough for her to be jealous and to want to claim her so other men knew she belonged to him. Not literally, of course. She didn't want to feel "possessed" by anyone, but it would be nice to be wanted on an exclusive basis.

When they arrived at the house, Cal glanced at his watch. "Your friend should be making an arrest about now."

A light dawned. "It's Edmund, isn't it? I should have known. As financial advisor to the tribal council, he knows everything about Chaco Canyon and how valuable the artifacts would be to unscrupulous collectors. I never felt really at ease around him. He was too…pushy."

"Let's get the steaks on," her brother suggested without agreeing or disagreeing with her conclusion.

"But Diana seems to like him," Julianne continued, worry for her friend swamping the relief that the case would soon be solved. "They sort of have a thing going."

"I noticed."

"Were you attracted to her?"

"I'm attracted to all beautiful women." His smile was cynical.

Cal started the gas grill, searched through her cabinets until he found a bottle of red wine, mixed a little marinade, then poured wine into two glasses and handed one to her.

She took a sip while studying her big brother. "Did someone hurt you, Cal?"

"Not me," he said, basting the steaks and turning them. "What are you going to fix to go with the meat?"

"Salads. I have some duchess potatoes in the freezer." She got busy with the rest of the meal while Cal took the steaks outside. By the time she had the table set for three and the meal was ready, she heard a vehicle.

Her heart thudded, sounding like a herd of wild mustangs stampeding through her chest. She went to the front door. "Oh," she murmured, unable to hide the disappointment.

Bruce Jones came to the door. "Hello, Julianne." He gave her a cheerful smile. "I saw your car when I passed by earlier and thought you might be alone tonight, but I see I'm too late. You already have company."

"My brother is here. Do you remember Cal from that summer we all went on the dig together?" She held the door open, inviting him inside.

"I do. He went off to college that fall and then on to law school while I finished my doctoral work."

She led the way to the kitchen and offered him a glass of wine. When Cal came inside, the two men shook hands. She wasn't sure what to do next. Since the table was set and the dinner ready, she invited the new guest to join them.

His gaze swept over the three settings, then her and her brother. "If you're sure," he said.

"We have plenty and I don't think our other guest is going to show up. Please, be seated."

The next hour turned out to be quite pleasant. They reminisced about the fun they'd had at the summer volunteer program at an Apache archeology site near the Texas border.

"Hot," Cal reminded them. "You could fry eggs on any flat rock. I couldn't believe we had volunteered for that."

"But there was the river to cool off in and the afternoon siestas while the sun was the hottest," Julianne said to him.

"And the scorpion that got in my tent," he added.

"And the music at night. I loved the sing-alongs."

Bruce laughed. "I remember my knees aching and the back of my neck getting sunburned."

After the meal, they went out on the patio to enjoy the breeze and the stars that filled the sky. The desert had cooled to a pleasant sixty-eight degrees. Julianne felt suspended in time as she waited to hear from Tony.

Finally, when she thought it long past time for Bruce to leave, she heard cars—more than one—stop at her house.

"I'll go see who it is." She leaped to her feet and dashed to the front door. "Tony," she said, unable to hide the smile that formed on her lips.

Her joy gave way to confusion as Chuck and another officer got out of a highway patrol car and were joined by two others who parked behind Tony's SUV.

"What's going on?" she asked, opening the screened door and standing on the tiny porch.

"Is Dr. Jones here?" Tony asked.

She glanced at Bruce's car. "Yes. He and Cal are on the patio. Why?"

Tony stopped in front of her, then with hands on her shoulders, gently led her to a chair. "Stay here," he said.

Bewildered, she asked, "Am I under arrest?"

He smiled and shook his head. "I'll explain later," he said.

He and Chuck went through the house to the back while the other three policemen circled around the outside of the cottage. Julianne followed Tony and Chuck.

"Hey, Tony," she heard Cal say. "You're late."

"There was a delay. Hello, Bruce," Tony said. "We got the men who were loading up a van at the museum."

Julianne peeked through the open door of the kitchen at the four men on the patio.

Bruce rose. "What?" he said in surprise. "You mean, someone was stealing from the museum? Tonight?"

"Right. The men you forced to do your dirty work for you. The Albuquerque police picked up your contact there, also the collector who got the other pieces."

"I don't know what you're talking about," Bruce said, sounding genuinely perplexed to Julianne.

What, she wondered, was Tony doing? Surely Bruce wouldn't steal and sell the prized antiques he'd spent so much effort on recovering from the ruins.

"I have one question," Tony said after Chuck cuffed her old family friend and told him his rights. "Why?"

In the soft light, she saw Bruce's face harden. "You'll soon have your Ph.D.," he said to Tony. "That and three jobs might be enough for you to live on if you don't have alimony and bills to pay, but don't count on it."

"I'll remember that," Tony said. He motioned to Chuck.

The highway patrolmen left with Bruce in handcuffs. Julianne sat very still in the dim living room as realization swept over her. Bruce was the ringleader. Bruce, who she'd known for years.

It felt like another betrayal.

She went out to the patio. "I want to know what's going on," she said. "*Now.*"

Chapter Thirteen

"Can you believe this heat when we're already in the middle of November?" Diana asked. She slipped into the chair opposite Julianne and picked up the menu.

Julianne pushed a wisp of hair behind her ear. "The weather report indicates it should break soon. Rain is heading inland from the Pacific."

"Secondhand weather," her friend groused. "California and Arizona get the coolness and the moisture first. We get anything that's left over."

Julianne laughed. "I've never looked at weather in quite that way."

Diana became serious. "It was good of your brother to take on Josiah's case pro bono. I found it hard to believe that Dr. Jones was the culprit. The noon report on the radio said he was indicted by the grand jury and that Josiah and his cousin will get parole rather than doing time."

Julianne reminded herself if Josiah had opened up and told the complete truth to begin with, he might not have been charged in the crime at all.

What the crooks hadn't known was that Tony and Chuck had the museum under tight security and that Tony had already noticed that the number of cataloged items from the site didn't match the number in the museum records. Bruce was changing the numbers and selling those pieces he left out of the inventory.

"Money," she said to Diana. "He thought he should get more money for his work."

"Huh. He shouldn't have gone into the field if he wanted to get rich."

"That's what I thought, too. It seems Bruce felt things were getting a little too hot when Tony started nosing around. He knew Josiah from the garage. He also knew Josiah's cousin worked at the Chaco site. Both had families and not much money."

Diana nodded. "They both had police records from their youths. Edmund said Dr. Jones used those facts as a hold over them, threatening to frame them. He planted a valuable pot at Josiah's home."

Julianne felt a twinge of guilt that she'd suspected Edmund of being part of the gang at times. "That sort of backfired," she said with a rueful grimace. "Josiah gave it and one of his pots to me as part payment for his son's delivery. Then he gave me the other pots to sell at Tony's place. Only, it was a sting operation and not part of Bruce's orders. They'd messed up the original delivery and thought this was a good way to get rid of the incriminating evidence. Tony had let it be known he was looking for 'good' stuff. The garage owner across the street from the shop had passed the info to Josiah."

"Pretty inept crooks when you think about it." Diana shook her head at the foibles of the pair, then peered at the menu. "Mmm, there's a salmon special. I'll have that."

"Me, too. Then I can feel virtuous when I order the pumpkin pie soufflé for dessert."

"Pumpkin? Isn't that a vegetable?" Diana asked with big-eyed innocence.

Julianne laughed. "I like the way you think."

Driving home after the pleasant Friday ritual of lunch, then grocery shopping, Julianne considered the past three weeks. She'd had to appear before the jury and tell everything she knew about the case, which had been pitifully little in the overall picture. As she'd told Tony at that first meeting, she'd only been the delivery service.

At the cottage she cleaned house and washed clothes, then changed to jogging shorts and an old T-shirt and set out for a run along the arroyo. Thirty minutes later she slowed to a walk and turned back toward home.

The exercise made her feel better and cleared her thinking somewhat. The quiet of the desert evening permeated her being and soothed her bruised heart. Thinking of Tony made her ache inside, and physical activity was the only thing that helped calm her spirits.

She wasn't looking forward to the following day. Chief Windover had declared a holiday in honor of Tony and Chuck for solving the case. She was included in the festivities.

She could hardly refuse to attend.

Saturday dawned clear and warm. At four, Julianne dressed in navy slacks and a navy, red and white knit shirt. She carried a red windbreaker in case the evening turned cool, and wore comfortable sneakers. There would be dancing by firelight later that night.

Today was the big celebration. The NAWAC ladies had planned a cookout. The new archeological dig at Chaco Canyon would be dedicated to the memory of the Ancient Ones. The site would then have dirt sprinkled in it as part of a ceremonial burial. The park service would cover it entirely during the following week.

She thought of all that Tony had told her when he showed her the artifacts after they'd gone to find Josiah and instead found the trailer gone.

A time for all things, he'd explained about the ruins. *Trees, villages, animals, people.*

In some ways, it was a comforting thought. All good things come to an end, he'd told her. But so did the bad ones. Life was an unpredictable mixture of both.

She drove to the park as sunset painted the sky in dreamy mauve backlighted by a golden lining. Dick Worth spotted her when she parked near the headquarters building and walked toward the picnic area.

"I'm glad you could make it," he said, falling into step with her.

She gave him a cheerful smile. "I wouldn't miss it. I love pit-roasted pork and fry bread. It was nice of you to provide the meat."

"The chief's cousin supervised while Tony and I did the grunt work."

Her heart tightened at Tony's name, but she entered the noisy throng around the fire pit with a calm, smiling manner.

Other than in court, she hadn't seen Tony since the arrest. It turned out that Bruce's mysterious appearance at her home was to establish an alibi for him while the museum was being looted of the new items they'd discovered.

She gave a little indignant huff. Not only had Bruce used her for an alibi, he'd eaten her food and drunk her wine as if he really were the old family friend he'd pretended to be that night.

Her nerves gave a gigantic lurch when she and Dick wound their way to the front of the crowd. The layers of sage and wet burlap were being lifted off the fire pit by two men. A third seemed to be in charge of the operation.

Julianne had to smile as Tony and Chuck obeyed the stream of directives in opening the pit and removing the roasted meat. When they at last lifted the pig free and clear, a cheer went up from the crowd.

Turning, Tony and Chuck took a bow, then used handkerchiefs to wipe the sweat from their faces.

She found herself laughing for no reason except everyone else was. The two men grinned and went to work cutting the meat under the direction of the supervising chef.

The park manager took her arm and brought her with him as he joined Chief Windover at a nearby table, which was obviously set up for the guests of honor.

"I shouldn't sit here," she murmured.

"Of course you should," the chief told her. "You're as much a hero as the men."

This was news to her. A faint tingle of alarm went through her as she wondered what the chief and park manager planned. There was a decided twinkle in their eyes.

When the pig was quartered satisfactorily, the three cooks gave up their places to several women from the local tribe and came over to the table.

Julianne's heart fluttered a little when Tony glanced at her and nodded. Outwardly she remained calm, cool and collected. Until she spotted her father winding his way through the happy throng.

"Dad," she said. "Cal." She glanced past her relatives. "Where's Sam?"

"He had to work," her father told her.

After introductions were made all around, Julianne sat between Tony and her father while they were served huge platters of pork, corn on the cob, beans flavored with jalapeño peppers and other mouthwatering food.

"I didn't know you two were coming," she said to her dad and brother.

"Chief Windover's secretary called," Cal explained. "She said the tribe wanted to honor you for your dedication to the health and welfare of their people."

"We wouldn't have missed it for the world," her father said with a delighted grin.

"Yeah, neither would I," she murmured, uneasy at being singled out for doing her job.

"I think it's just going to be a speech," Tony said as if aware of her discomfort.

For the first time, she let herself meet his gaze. She quickly looked away. He was so handsome it took her breath.

His low laughter had the same effect, she found. She turned to her father. "Are you two staying with me tonight?"

Her dad nodded. "If you don't mind. We have to get back early tomorrow, though. The university is holding a workshop for PE teachers this weekend."

"And I have a date tomorrow night," Cal said.

Julianne clasped her hands over her heart. "What poor woman have you convinced to go out with you?"

He grinned. "You think I'd tell you or Sam? No way."

When the meal was finished, the chief rose and called for quiet. He spoke of the ancient culture and the importance of one's ancestors. He told them that the research dig was complete.

A tribal shaman sprinkled crystals into the fire that caused it to flare and spark for a moment. He sang to the four winds and asked the blessings of the Ancient Ones on everyone there.

Afterward, Chief Windover presented tribal masks to Tony and Chuck that would keep evil from their homes. Then he beckoned Julianne to come to him.

When she stood beside him, he told the crowd of her work for the people and particularly of her concern for Josiah and his family. He told her the tribal council wanted to give her something very special.

To her consternation, he presented her with the corrugated pot that Josiah had given her. Before she could protest such a valuable gift, he continued, "This is a replica of the ancient artifact. The real piece will be kept at the museum with a sign that says it is on permanent loan from the collection of

Julianne Martin." He handed her the replica. "This one is for your home, a vessel to store many happy memories in throughout your life."

After thanking the chief and tribal council, she returned to her seat among cheers from the crowd.

When the twilight deepened, the fire was rekindled in the pit and dancing began. Julianne and Cal joined in. They'd grown up with Native American friends and were at ease with the joyful custom.

Glancing up, she saw Tony's eyes on her while he and her father chatted like old friends. The dancing flames in the fire pit seemed to glow in those dark depths, adding a promise of passion and magic that thrummed through her like the insistent beat of the ceremonial drums.

Before the evening was over, he joined her in a circle dance. She loved the feel of her hand in his as they moved around and around with the other dancers, the heat of desire in her blood while longing filled her heart.

Julianne was sad to see her father and brother leave right after breakfast on Sunday morning.

She waved until they were well down the road. Returning inside, she stopped before the armoire she used as a sideboard and studied the intricate piece of pottery with the raised dots. She truly was honored that the original was in the museum as a gift from her.

Tony and Chuck had donated their masks to the museum, too. Although they weren't ancient, they were of museum quality and handmade by an important tribal shaman. It had been a nice gesture. All in all, the evening had been very pleasant.

The only thing that could have made it better was...

No, she wouldn't think of Tony and how it had felt to be near him. She sighed and decided to walk while the morning was cool.

Today she didn't have to go to the clinic. All the paperwork and computer input was done, thanks to the two students who came in for two hours during the afternoons. She and Edmund had even found the money to pay them a small salary for their work.

Putting her thoughts on hold, she hurried the last mile back to her home. Near the house, she stopped and surveyed the patio. Someone was there.

Through the bird-of-paradise bush growing beside the arbor, she spotted movement. A man dressed in a white shirt and jeans leaned against the framing and stared out at the dry wash and the desert beyond.

Inhaling deeply, Julianne went forward. "Hello," she called as she crossed the creek pebbles that covered the backyard and kept the dust under control.

Tony swung his head in her direction and observed her approach. "Hello yourself," he said when she stopped at the edge of the flagstones before stepping on the patio.

She stood there feeling awkward and unkempt. "Are you done with the proceedings in Bruce's case?" She knew he and Chuck had been busy working with the D.A.'s office to present evidence to the court.

"Yeah. It'll be a few months before his trial comes up. He's out on bail."

"Oh. Should I be worried?"

The handsome face took on a threatening expression. "I don't think he'll bother you. He's a thief, not a murderer."

"That's a relief," she quipped.

He frowned at her.

She tensed, expecting bad news for some reason.

"You got any plans for the day?"

Surprised she shook her head.

"You want to go to the canyon and see the ruins once more before they're covered?"

"Yes, I would."

They were mostly silent on the trip. When they arrived, Tony took her hand and led her past the rocky debris to the new dig, as he had the first time they came out here.

A couple of birds jumped from branch to branch in a chokecherry tree, searching for any berries that had been overlooked. After they flew off, the canyon was eerily quiet, with only the whisper of the wind in the cottonwoods.

"Listen," Tony said.

Above the rustle of the leaves, she heard the soft murmurs from the past—children's voices that seemed joyful, other, older ones that were sad. They spoke of lives lived to their full here in this place but in another time.

Giving a tug on her hand, Tony led the way to a vantage point where they could survey the ruins. They sat on a large boulder, and she was aware of his heat along her left side.

"Tomorrow this will be gone," he said, "buried again so that no one will be able to tell that once people walked here, that once there were houses and streets and farms all along the canyon, that once laughter echoed from that cliff. Once, long ago."

She thought her own heart might be buried here, too, but she couldn't tell him that. She nodded.

"Julianne," he said in the softest tone.

She glanced at him, then couldn't look away.

"I asked you out here for a reason."

"What reason?" she forced herself to ask and gazed at him with the bright-eyed interest of the ground squirrel who spied on them from a niche between two rocks.

A smile lifted the corners of his mouth for a second, then disappeared. He solemnly studied her face.

He was leaving. That's what he wanted to tell her. His job here was done and he was being assigned to another case in another area.

Her heart stopped, then beat again, heavy now, like a death knell. She tried to appear composed, interested in his news, pleased for him. Maybe he even got a promotion out of the case no one had been able to solve for over a year.

"Dick Worth has asked me to take over as his assistant with an eye toward being the district park manager when he retires. What do you think?"

The news was so unexpected she really couldn't think for a moment. "That, that sounds…great. If that's what you want." She peered at him. "Is it?"

A wonderful smile spread slowly over his face. "Yes."

She nodded, unable to think past this news.

"I want to stay," he murmured, "because this is where you are, and where you are is where I want to be."

Frowning, she tried to make sense of this, in view of her expectation that he was leaving. "How nice," she said politely, then, "What does that mean?"

Tony saw that he'd managed to totally confuse her. Well, join the crowd. He was rather confused—no, not confused, not in his feelings, but how to say what he meant.

"Jules," he began.

She clasped her hands in her lap and stared at them. He put his hand over both of hers.

"I've fallen for you. In a big way," he added while she stared at him dumbfounded.

"You love me?"

He nodded. "A lot." Talking got easier after admitting the truth. "Will you marry me?"

"I don't know. I haven't thought about marriage. I mean, I have, but I...I thought you brought me here to tell me you were leaving."

"I couldn't leave, not without you." He leaned his head down until he could touch his temple to hers.

Tears brought a silver sheen to her eyes. He touched her eyelashes with one finger.

"I didn't mean to make you cry." He began to feel a bit uncertain. "You've got to tell me how you feel. Am I wrong to think you might love me back?"

"Oh, no, you're not wrong, not at all."

"Ah, Jules," he said on a relieved breath.

"Tony, oh, Tony."

She said his name several times and kissed his face wherever she could reach. He lifted her into his lap to make it easier.

"I love you," he said, feeling completely free to hold her close, to touch her, to know she loved him, too.

They sealed their love with a kiss...a very long, very passionate kiss. He wanted to make love to her, but there was time for that, he realized, lots of time for everything that was to come.

Julianne smiled at him. It was a smile to warm up the coldest heart, to soothe the most restless of spirits. It was a smile meant for him...just him.

The wind blew down the canyon, coming from

the north, whispering of winter, but he wasn't worried. He would always bask in the sweet glow of Julianne's love.

Julianne.

Beloved.

* * * * *

The story of the Aquilon family continues in
CANYON COUNTRY,
the new miniseries from reader favorite
LAURIE PAIGE.
Don't miss ACQUIRING MR. RIGHT.
On sale November 2006.

*Set in darkness beyond the ordinary world.
Passionate tales of life and death.
With characters' lives ruled by laws the everyday
world can't begin to imagine.*

*Introducing NOCTURNE, a spine-tingling new
line from Silhouette Books.*

*The thrills and chills begin with
UNFORGIVEN by Lindsay McKenna*

Plucked from the depths of hell, former military sharpshooter Reno Manchahi was hired by the government to kill a thief, but he had a mission of his own. Descended from a family of shape-shifters, Reno vowed to get the revenge he'd thirsted for all these years. But his mission went awry when his target turned out to be a powerful seductress, Magdalena Calen Hernandez, who risked everything to battle a potent evil. Suddenly, Reno had to transform himself into a true hero and fight the enemy that threatened them all. He had to become a Warrior for the Light....

*Turn the page for a sneak preview of
UNFORGIVEN by Lindsay McKenna.
On sale September 26 wherever books are sold.*

Chapter 1

One shot...one kill.

The sixteen-pound sledgehammer came down with such fierce power that the granite boulder shattered instantly. A spray of glittering mica exploded into the air and sparkled momentarily around the man who wielded the tool as if it were a weapon. Sweat ran in rivulets down Reno Manchahi's drawn, intense face. Naked from the waist up, the hot July sun beating down on his back, he hefted the sledgehammer skyward once more. Muscles in his thick forearms leaped and biceps bulged. Even his breath was focused on the boulder. In his mind's eye, he pictured Army General Robert Hampton's fleshy, arrogant fifty-year-old features on the rock's surface. Air exploded from between his lips as he brought the avenging hammer down. The boulder pulverized beneath his funneled hatred.

One shot...one kill...

Nostrils flaring, he inhaled the dank, humid heat and drew it deep into his massive lungs. Revenge allowed Reno to endure his imprisonment at a U.S. Navy brig near San Diego, California. Drops of sweat were flung in all directions as the crack of his sledgehammer claimed a third stone victim. Mouth taut, Reno moved to the next boulder.

The other prisoners in the stone yard gave him a wide berth. They always did. They instinctively felt his simmering hatred, the palpable revenge in his cinnamon-colored eyes, was more than skin-deep.

And they whispered he was different.

Reno enjoyed being a loner for good reason. He came from a medicine family of shape-shifters. But even this secret power had not protected him—or his family. His wife, Ilona, and his three-year-old daughter, Sarah, were dead. Murdered by Army General Hampton in their former home on USMC base in Camp Pendleton, California. Bitterness thrummed through Reno as he savagely pushed the toe of his scarred leather boot against several smaller pieces of gray granite that were in his way.

The sun beat down upon Manchahi's naked shoulders, grown dark red over time, shouting his half-

Apache heritage. With his straight black hair grazing his thick shoulders, copper skin and broad face with high cheekbones, everyone knew he was Indian. When he'd first arrived at the brig, some of the prisoners taunted him and called him Geronimo. Something strange happened to Reno during his fight with the name-calling prisoners. Leaning down after he'd won the scuffle, he'd snarled into each of their bloodied faces that if they were going to call him anything, they would call him *gan,* which was the Apache word for *devil.*

His attackers had been shocked by the wounds on their faces, the deep claw marks. Reno recalled doubling his fist as they'd attacked him en masse. In that split second, he'd gone into an altered state of consciousness. In times of danger, he transformed into a jaguar. A deep, growling sound had emitted from his throat as he defended himself in the three-against-one fracas. It all happened so fast that he thought he had imagined it. He'd seen his hands morph into a forearm and paw, claws extended. The slashes left on the three men's faces after the fight told him he'd begun to shape-shift. A fist made bruises and swelling; not four perfect, deep claw marks. Stunned and anxious, he hid the knowledge of what else he was from these prisoners. Reno's only defense was to make all the prisoners so damned scared of him and remain a loner.

Alone. Yeah, he was alone, all right. The steel

hammer swept downward with hellish ferocity. As the granite groaned in protest, Reno shut his eyes for just a moment. Sweat dripped off his nose and square chin.

Straightening, he wiped his furrowed, wet brow and looked into the pale blue sky. What got his attention was the startling cry of a red-tailed hawk as it flew over the brig yard. Squinting, he watched the bird. Reno could make out the rust-colored tail on the hawk. As a kid growing up on the Apache reservation in Arizona, Reno knew that all animals that appeared before him were messengers.

Brother, what message do you bring me? Reno knew one had to ask in order to receive. Allowing the sledgehammer to drop to his side, he concentrated on the hawk who wheeled in tightening circles above him.

Freedom! the hawk cried in return.

Reno shook his head, his black hair moving against his broad, thickset shoulders. *Freedom? No way, Brother. No way.* Figuring that he was making up the hawk's shrill message, Reno turned away. Back to his rocks. Back to picturing Hampton's smug face.

Freedom!

Look for UNFORGIVEN by Lindsay McKenna,
the spine-tingling launch title
from Silhouette Nocturne™.
Available September 26 wherever books are sold.

Silhouette® Desire®

**Introducing an exciting appearance
by legendary
New York Times bestselling author**

DIANA PALMER
HEARTBREAKER

He's the ultimate bachelor…
but he may have just met
the one woman to change his ways!

Join the drama in the story of a confirmed
bachelor, an amnesiac beauty and their
unexpected passionate romance.

"Diana Palmer is a mesmerizing storyteller
who captures the essence of what
a romance should be."—*Affaire de Coeur*

**Heartbreaker *is available from Silhouette Desire
in September 2006.***

Those sexy Irishmen are back!

Bestselling author

Kate Hoffmann

is joining the Harlequin Blaze line—and she's
brought her bestselling Temptation miniseries,
THE MIGHTY QUINNS, with her.
Because these guys are definitely Blaze-worthy....

All Quinn males, past and present, know the legend
of the first Mighty Quinn. And they've all been
warned about the family curse—that the only thing
capable of bringing down a Quinn is a woman.
Still, the last three Quinn brothers never guess
that lying low could be so sensually satisfying....

The Mighty Quinns: Marcus, on sale October 2006
The Mighty Quinns: Ian, on sale November 2006
The Mighty Quinns: Declan, on sale December 2006

Don't miss it!

Available wherever Harlequin books are sold.

SPECIAL EDITION™

Experience the "magic" of falling in love at Halloween with a new *Holiday Hearts* story!

UNDER HIS SPELL

by *KRISTIN HARDY*

October 2006

Bad-boy ski racer J. J. Cooper can get any woman he wants—except Lainie Trask. Lainie's grown up with him and vows that nothing he says or does will change her mind. But J.J.'s got his eye on Lainie, and when he moves into her neighborhood and into her life, she finds herself falling under his spell....

THE PART-TIME WIFE

by *USA TODAY* bestselling author

Maureen Child

Abby Talbot was the belle of Eastwick society;
the perfect hostess and wife. If only her
husband were more attentiive. But when
she sets out to teach him a lesson and files
for divorce, Abby quickly learns her husband's
true identity...and exposes them to scandals
and drama galore!

On sale October 2006 from Silhouette Desire!

*Available wherever books are sold,
including most bookstores, supermarkets,
discount stores and drug stores.*

SPECIAL EDITION

#1783 IT TAKES A FAMILY—Victoria Pade
Northbridge Nuptials
Penniless and raising an infant niece after her sister's death, Karis Pratt's only hope was to go to Northbridge, Montana, and find the baby's father, Luke Walker. Did this small-town cop hold the key to renewed family ties and a bright new future for Karis?

#1784 ROCK-A-BYE RANCHER—Judy Duarte
When rugged Clay Callaghan asked attorney Dani De La Cruz to help bring his orphaned granddaughter back from Mexico, Dani couldn't say no to the case…but what would she say to the smitten cattleman's more personal proposals?

#1785 MOTHER IN TRAINING—Marie Ferrarella
Talk of the Neighborhood
When Zooey Finnegan walked out on her fiancé, the gossips pounced. Unfazed, she went on to work wonders as nanny to widower Jack Lever's two kids. But when she got Jack to come out of his own emotional shell...the town *really* had something to talk about!

#1786 UNDER HIS SPELL—Kristin Hardy
Holiday Hearts
Lainie Trask's longtime crush on J. J. Cooper hadn't amounted to much—J.J. seemed too busy with World Cup skiing and womanizing to notice the feisty curator. But an injury led to big changes for J.J.—including plenty of downtime to discover Lainie's charms….

#1787 LOVE LESSONS—Gina Wilkins
Medical researcher Dr. Catherine Travis had all the trappings of the good life…except for someone special to share it with. Would maintenance man and part-time college student Mike Clancy fix what ailed the good doctor…despite the odds arrayed against them?

#1788 NOT YOUR AVERAGE COWBOY—
Christine Wenger
When rancher Buck Porter invited famous cookbook author and city slicker Merry Turner to help give Rattlesnake Ranch a makeover, it was a recipe for trouble. So what was the secret ingredient that soon made the cowboy, his young daughter and Merry inseparable?